Something to Say

Also by Lisa Moore Ramée
A Good Kind of Trouble

Something to Say

LISA MOORE RAMÉE

Illustrations by Bre Indigo

Balzer + Bray

An Imprint of HarperCollins*Publishers*

Balzer + Bray is an imprint of HarperCollins Publishers.

Something to Say
Text copyright © 2020 by Lisa Moore Ramée
Interior illustrations copyright © 2020 by Bre Indigo

ISBN 978-0-06-283671-7

20 21 22 23 24   PC/LSCH   10 9 8 7 6 5 4 3 2 1
❖
First Edition

For Mamasita Baunita—no love is bigger

And for Grandpa, who never met a Western he didn't like

1
NOT LIKE ANYONE ELSE

Mama gets home from work earlier than usual, and even though I shut my laptop quick and slide it under a couch cushion, it's too late.

"Hi, Mama," I say innocently, raising my voice so she can hear me over my grandpa Gee's blaring television. A rickety fan in the corner of the living room is blowing a steady breeze at me, but I'm still hot and my legs stick to the leather couch.

Mama clanks her purse and keys down on the small table by the front door. "Oh, don't even try it, Jenae," she says, and points at the cushion. "Move that before someone sits on it."

Guiltily, I pull my computer out. Mama isn't a fan of my shiny silver laptop. Mostly because my dad bought it. Anything that makes her think of him is never going to be good. She's always talking about what he should or shouldn't do, but she never says it would be better if he came by more. I guess I'm the only one who thinks that.

I try not to care too much. He's an actor and travels all over the place making movies, so he's really busy. And in interviews he always says he has a daughter, so it's not as if he has forgotten about me.

Mama walks over to Gee. "Hey, Daddy," she says, and gives him a kiss on the top of his head, then reaches over, grabs the remote, and turns down the volume.

"Hey, yourself," Gee says, not turning his head away from the old Western movie he's watching. As soon as Mama leaves the room, he'll crank the volume right back up. Gee's hearing isn't great, but he refuses to get hearing aids, so when he's home, we all have to suffer with the TV volume set to ear-piercing loud.

Mama frowns at me, which is not so unusual. Sometimes when Mama looks at me, I can tell she does not like what she sees. She doesn't understand how her daughter could turn out so different from her. But I'm not like anyone. And I'm all right with that. Being unique should be a good thing, but the world is full of people like Mama who think fitting in is more important than being yourself.

"I told your father buying you that thing was a bad idea," Mama says. "Just plain ridiculous, encouraging you—"

"Do you not see me trying to watch my program?" Gee hollers, cutting off Mama and gesturing at the TV. "If y'all want to be chatty, get on out of here."

Mama knows better than to argue with her father, so she raises her perfectly threaded eyebrows and beckons for me to follow her into the kitchen. She likes to complain that Gee still treats her like a baby, but it's his house, so he makes the rules.

We live here because the house is huge, and with Nana June gone, he'd get lonely.

My grandmother didn't die, she just decided she was tired of Gee—of all men actually—and moved to Florida to live with her best friend. She sends me neon T-shirts all the time that say things like *Live Your Best Life!* and *Nothing's Impossible!* I don't think Nana June gets how hard it is to live your own life when you're only eleven. People steady want to tell you what to do.

Mama clicks across the hardwood floor in her high heels, and I peel myself off the couch. As soon as I get in the kitchen, she starts up.

"Your father gave you that computer so you could do your *homework*, not watch that foolishness."

That foolishness is what Mama calls Astrid Dane, my favorite YouTube show. "It's summer, Mama. I don't have any homework." I don't bother arguing that Astrid Dane is not foolishness, because Mama has her mind made up about that. Mama likes "real" things, nothing make-believe. Astrid Dane is a twelve-year-old immortal girl who has all sorts of ghosts living inside her, and they take over her personality sometimes, and that is just about as far from real as you can get—according to Mama.

But I love Astrid Dane.

Mama crosses her arms tight against her chest and stares at me. "What exactly are you wearing?" Her tone implies I am wearing my panties on my head.

I look down at myself as if I don't remember what I have on. "Just . . . a v-vest I made?" I can't help my voice going up

at the end. Nana June taught me how to sew. I can't do a whole bunch, but a vest is pretty easy. And this one is great. It's an exact copy of what Astrid Dane wore in the "Corruption" episode. I paid attention to every detail, even getting the elephant buttons right.

"Lord, girl," Mama starts, and I know nothing good is going to come after that. "How're you going to have any friends if you walk around in crazy costumes?"

I don't answer. And not because I don't want friends. But I don't *need* them the way some people do. Especially if what I wear is going to matter to them. Mama acts as if that means there is something wrong with me.

The kitchen door gets pushed open, and my brother, Malcolm, crutches in. He's been on crutches since his surgery a few weeks ago. "You really need to come home and start hollering like that?" he asks Mama. Malcolm's not afraid to talk back to Mama like I am. Maybe because he's older, but probably even when I'm grown and not living with Mama anymore, I'll still be scared to speak my mind.

Mama puts her hands on her hips. "How come you didn't start dinner?" she asks Malcolm, and I feel guilty right away. Even though it's Malcolm's turn to cook, I should've done it. Especially since his injury is all my fault.

2

A PLAN

Mama glares at Malcolm. "You can't just sit up in your room all day, listening to music and not doing nothing else," she says. "Tonight is your turn. You know that."

"It's too hard," Malcolm says. "Standing up that long hurts." He moves the leg with the big black brace out in front of him, as if Mama might've forgotten about his injury.

Mama doesn't even look at Malcolm's leg; she just leans against the island and puts her hands on her hips. "The doctors cleared you for regular activity. Seems to me if they said you could drive, you sure enough can stand up and cook some dinner. I've told you, you need to help out here. I'm sure not going to just watch you turn out like these *supposed*-to-be men."

She's dragging both Malcolm's dad and mine with that comment. Malcolm's dad is Mama's first husband, and mine is her second. After two marriages and two divorces, Mama has sworn off men forever. Maybe when your heart gets broken twice, it doesn't ever fit right back together.

"I'm not going to, Mama. Can you please give me a break?" Malcolm asks.

"I'll give you a break when you explain your plan to me," Mama says. "You got one yet?"

She's been asking Malcolm this question since his surgery.

Malcolm shrugs. "I don't know." He sounds so sad when he says it that I have to look away. Ever since he was my age, Malcolm had such a clear plan. A total slam dunk. Be the best point guard in his high school league, get recruited by a Division I college, get drafted into the NBA, make millions and buy Mama a mansion. (Mama always laughed at that part of Malcolm's plan and said she had no use for a house that big.) But that was before. Before he tore his ACL *and* meniscus. And had to have surgery.

"That's not good enough, Malcolm," Mama says.

I don't like when Mama gets on Malcolm's case, but if she knew I was the reason Malcolm was home with a busted-up knee instead of still playing college basketball, she'd definitely go back to yelling at me.

Gee always says, *You break it, you buy it*, which is his way of saying you have to take ownership of your mistakes and figure out a way to fix them. Since I'm the one who broke Malcolm, I have to make him better, but I sure don't know how. So far, I've tried doing his chores, buying him sunflower seeds, and staying out of his way. None of that worked. Malcolm's not the only one who needs a plan.

"That assistant coach, Coach Naz, called me again," Mama says. "He reminded me you still haven't registered for classes. You know they don't *have* to renew your scholarship."

Malcolm mumbles something, and it sounds a whole lot like he said he didn't care. But I know that's not the truth.

Mama stares at him and her face is stone hard, but then it softens just a little. "Malcolm. You need to care. This is your life. Basketball was only one ticket to the ride. Whether you can play or not, they're still willing to pay for school. You're going to let that opportunity slip away? You know how few Black young men are even *getting* college degrees?"

When Malcolm doesn't answer, Mama throws up her hands in frustration. "Well, one of you needs to get some dinner started. I'm going upstairs to change."

When she leaves the kitchen, as nicely as I can, I ask Malcolm, "You want to help me make something?" He and I used to cook together before he went away to school. It was a lot of fun. Maybe cooking with me will start to make him feel better, but he shakes his head.

"Naw," he says, and crutches out of the kitchen.

I open the refrigerator and stare dismally at the food, hoping something interesting will come to me. What am I supposed to make? Then the door pushes open, and I think it's going to be Malcolm, changing his mind, but it's Gee.

He walks over, reaches into the fridge, and grabs a package of chicken. "You know, Nae-nae," he says as he gets some seasonings out of the cupboard, "it's important to respect your mama, but don't be afraid of using your voice. God gave you a brain for a reason. Gave you a mouth too. Don't be afraid to speak up."

Easy for him to say. Gee's not afraid of anything. I'm afraid of more things than I can count.

3

TOO SOON

The first day of school comes too soon, and I'm trying to hold it off by savoring a piece of cinnamon toast. Until today I've been excited about starting junior high. Elementary school was okay, but it was starting to feel like a shirt that had gotten shrunk in the wash. Tight around the neck and arms; too snug and short. I figured junior high might be more comfortable. More space to spread out and find a nice empty spot to fade into. But now that the first day is here, I'm nervous. There will be a bunch of people I don't know. And they'll need to put me in some kind of box, the way people like to do. Everyone thinks you're supposed to fit in somewhere. Be a *type* of thing. I just want to be left alone.

"It's about time to go, Jenae," Mama says, and jangles her keys at me. "Big day."

"I just need to grab my bag, and then I'm ready." Some crumbs and butter slide down my chin, and I wipe them off with the back of my hand.

"Why aren't you wearing that new sweatshirt we got? It's

cute, and it cost a grip too, so don't be telling me it doesn't fit right."

The amount of glitter on that sweatshirt should be illegal. "I want to save it. Not look like I was trying too hard on the first day?" I meant to say it like a statement, sound strong, but it's hard to give that attitude when Mama is looking at me like I don't make any sense. Like I'm the wrong-shaped piece in the puzzle she's trying to put together.

"Go on and get your bag, then," Mama says.

I rush upstairs. I still can't believe I have it. An Astrid Dane bag. And Mama doesn't even know. When we went school-clothes shopping, I saw it just hanging there on a wall of backpacks. A pale yellow messenger-style bag with tiny clocks. It doesn't say Astrid Dane on it—luckily, or Mama never would've let me get it—but a true Astrid Dane fan would know. I had to act casual, like I didn't care whether I got it or not. Mama humphed at the price but then said okay.

I sling the bag over my shoulder and stare at myself in my mirror. Mama acts like new clothes are going to change my life, but I don't think they make a difference. All I see is plain old me. Brown skin. Poufy hair. Wide brown eyes. Short. Pokey elbows and knees, but a pudgy middle. The bag doesn't make me look any different either, but it makes me feel better. Like maybe junior high won't crush me.

"Jenae!" Mama calls from downstairs, and I hustle out of my room, but when I pass by Malcolm's door, I can hear the pulsing *boom, bah, boom* of one of his hip-hop songs, so I know he's awake. I wish there weren't any sounds coming from his room. It should be silent. And he should still be away at college. Happy and whole.

But I ruined everything.

Watching him lying on the basketball court, rocking back in forth in pain, was probably the worst thing I've ever seen. I had wanted him home so badly. The thought had blasted out of me. *COME HOME.* I should've known thinking that super hard would cause something awful to happen. I should've learned from the first time.

I knock on his door, and his music goes off and he says, "What?"

I open the door slowly. Malcolm's room isn't tidy like mine. His room is a mess. Clothes are all over the floor, and dirty plates are on his dresser. His trash can is overflowing, and honestly, his room stinks. Mama must never come in here, because she would throw a fit if she knew how gross it was.

"I'm leaving for school," I say. "I just wanted to say bye."

Malcolm's lying in bed like it's the weekend. "Remember what I told you," he says. "Cafeterias are for chumps. Eat outside. Like in the quad, all right?"

Malcolm took me around the school last week so I would know where all my classes were. It made me feel bad, because I'm trying to fix him; he's not supposed to be helping me.

"I'll eat outside," I say, not admitting I have no plans to sit in the quad. I try to think of something, anything I could say to make him feel like getting started on a new plan. "Malcolm,

I . . ." I can't think of a solitary thing.

Maybe he knows I have nothing to offer, because he doesn't even ask me what I was going to say. He just turns his music back on and grimaces as he gets into a different position.

"You better get going," he says, and almost smiles at me. I miss Malcolm's smiles.

I leave his room disappointed with myself. How am I going to make him better? I can't even think of how to get him out of bed.

The house is strangely quiet as I make my way downstairs. Gee is retired from his job as a mail carrier, but he still likes to get up early, and as soon as he is dressed and has had his cup of coffee (with so much sugar it's even too sweet for me), he starts in television watching. But he left for Las Vegas last night.

Mama had tons to say about "old folks driving late at night," but that didn't stop Gee. He has two favorite things: watching Westerns and getting the heck out of Dodge. That's what Gee calls it when he takes one of his trips, or even when he just takes a walk around the block. He says someone who spent as much time walking around outside as he did, delivering mail, has to get going every once in a while. It's no big surprise that his expression about getting out of Dodge comes straight from old Westerns.

Even though when he's home he tries to rupture our eardrums with the volume of the TV, as soon as he's gone the house is too still. Like it's holding its breath, just waiting for him to come back.

4

THE WAY IT USED TO BE

When we get to the first main street, as soon as Mama puts on her blinker to turn left, my chest squeezes in. I look behind us, at the way we used to go when I was still in elementary school. I wipe the sweat off my nose and face back around, watching the road coming at us.

Mama always drives me to school to make sure I'm not late (and so I don't get sweaty), but she lets me walk home. It's not very far, so before I'm ready, Mama's joining the long line of cars pulling into the drop-off zone.

A bunch of people are lined up along the zone, handing out fliers to all the drivers.

"Now what is this foolishness?" Mama mutters, and pushes the button to lower her window. A tall woman with a face full of freckles smiles and hands Mama the bright blue piece of paper.

I see SAY NO TO NAME CHANGE! written big and bold on the top.

"Ain't people got better things to do?" Mama says once the woman steps away from our car.

"What's it about?" I ask, trying to read the paper that's getting all crumpled in Mama's hand.

We're waiting for our turn to move up in the drop-off line, so Mama glances at the flier.

"Mm," she says, and shakes her head. "Looks like folks are talking about changing the name of the school."

A driver behind us toots their horn, and Mama turns and glares at them and then she moves up.

"Gee's not going to like that," I say. My school's name is John Wayne Junior High. It's named after a movie star who lived a long time ago. He made a whole bunch of Western movies, so of course my grandpa loves him. John Wayne movies are probably his favorite. Gee calls him the Duke.

"Shoot, it probably won't happen. Not with all these people having a conniption over it," Mama says. We've reached the drop-off area, so Mama leans over, putting her cheek close to me. "Go ahead and get going before you're late."

I give her a kiss goodbye, making sure I don't smudge her makeup, take a deep breath, and climb out of the car.

There's so much buzzy energy around me, I feel like I'm about to get stung. All sorts of people laughing and calling out to each other and doing coordinated clapping dance moves. It is not at all hard to imagine that I have landed on an alien planet.

Girls hug and act like they haven't seen each other in years. No one rushes up to me to give me a hug. No one even sees me. And I'm totally fine with that.

5

NOT A DANISH

I walk so slowly to my first period, I get to class just before the tardy bell.

"Take your seat, please," our history teacher, Mrs. Crawford, says, sighing at me, like she's already convinced I'm going to be a problem. She points to a desk in the very back.

That's exactly where I want to sit. Just because I'm quiet, people think I'm going to be one of those teacher's-pet-type kids, sitting in the front row, raising my hand all the time, and having my homework all ready to turn in. Mama gets mad when she sees a bunch of Satisfactories on my report cards instead of Excellents, as if "satisfactory" is a bad thing.

I shuffle to the back and take the seat next to Geoffrey Mingus. He doesn't look up. Geoffrey and I have gone to school together since kindergarten, but I think I'm the only one of us who knows that.

On the other side of me is a boy I don't know. He has red hair that is so bright it practically burns my eyes. Red hair isn't all that unusual, but this shade is. What's even more unusual is even though the boy is light-skinned, he's definitely Black, and I've never known anyone Black to have hair that color. I mean, it's the princess-in-*Brave* red.

He also has a yellow messenger bag with little clocks on it.

I swallow so hard, I almost choke. I set my bag on the floor on Geoffrey's side, not wanting red-hair boy to see it. It feels awkward, like we know each other somehow.

He's smiling at me so big it freaks me out, so I ignore him and pull out my notebook and pencil.

Red Hair taps my desk. "What's your name?"

I look over at Geoffrey. Maybe he told Red Hair to bother me, but Geoffrey doesn't seem like he's paying attention to me or anything else. He is slouched in his seat, rubbing one of his ears and making little *ch-ch-ch* sounds to whatever music must be rolling around in his head.

"Jenae," I say as softly as I can, but Mrs. Crawford still glares at me. It's as if Red Hair turned a big spotlight on me.

I adjust my ponytail, and sweat sprouts in my underarms. Darn. I'm a big-time sweater. Like seriously. And Mama was nice enough to tell me I have stinky stress sweat, and not even Mitchum deodorant for men kills it.

I have to get to the bathroom quick and use the wipes Mama pushed into my bag, before the stink latches onto me and has me labeled with some awful nickname. It's hard to stay invisible if funk is following you everywhere you go.

I'm certain it's too early in the period for me to get excused to the bathroom. I slow my breathing and try to calm myself in the hope that if I stop stressing, I'll stop stinking.

Red Hair is drawing instead of taking notes, and I can't help glancing at his paper, and am shocked and a little amazed that not only is he drawing a picture of Astrid Dane, but it's also actually *good*. He's got her massive explosion of hair and wide eyes, and sneaky smile.

Whoa. I wish I could draw her like that. He catches me looking, and my face gets boiling hot, like I was caught cheating or something.

When the bell rings, I pack up fast and get out of there. Since there's only a few minutes between classes, and I have to make a quick trip to the bathroom to freshen up, I need to hustle.

Red Hair follows me, and he's way too close.

"Jenae," he says, and I'm so shocked I forget to keep moving.

"Oof," he says when he smacks right into me. "You're fast."

I wait for him to say something else.

His grin is so big it covers his whole freckled face. And his light brown eyes are shining at me like maybe we know something about each other.

"I saw your bag! Astrid Dane, right? I didn't know there'd be another Danish here!"

I don't like the name for people who like Astrid Dane. Danish is a dumb thing to be called. Astrid does like her pastries, but she eats *doughnuts*. I have never once seen her eat a Danish. So really the only thing I can say is "I'm not a Danish." And then I hightail it away from him and do the thing I promised myself a million times I wouldn't do again, after I hurt Malcolm; I blast Red Hair as hard as I can with my thoughts. *GO AWAY! GO AWAY!*

Right before I push the bathroom door open, I glance over my shoulder, and he is gone. I feel relieved and sick at the same time. I did it again.

6

MIND CONTROL

I know it sounds ridiculous to say I can control people with my mind, and I wouldn't believe it either if I hadn't seen it happen. Twice. The first time, I was only five years old, so I couldn't be sure, but the second time—when I hurt Malcolm—I knew for certain what I could do.

When Malcolm first went away to college, I was so busy being proud of him that it took me a while to realize I missed him. When he first left, he'd Skype with us, but then he got too busy.

Mama would get so excited if one of his games was televised, but after the first few games, I didn't want to watch anymore. I didn't want to see how happy he was without me. Then, one night, while we were watching him on TV, all the sadness and anger and worry and everything just blasted out of me and right at Malcolm. But I never wanted him to get hurt. It seemed like it took forever for the coach and one of his teammates to get him up off the floor.

Bad things happen when I beam a thought out like that, and I should've known better.

When Malcolm had to come home to have surgery, I felt so guilty, I could barely look at him.

And now I've done it again.

Still, when I leave the bathroom, I'm relieved Red Hair hasn't rematerialized. I slink to second period, keeping my head down and staying out of people's way.

I get through second, third, and fourth period without getting called on, or picked on, and no red-haired pest tries to shine a spotlight on me. Being invisible isn't as hard as you might think. People don't see what they don't want to.

Lunch is after fourth period. I didn't explain to Malcolm, but the quad—with all its eighth graders and noise—was not where I wanted to be. I scoped out the perfect place while he was taking me around. Way across the field, behind a huge metal storage container. It has a first aid symbol on it, so I'm sure it's where they keep all the emergency supplies. Sitting behind the container is the perfect lunch spot. I'm not hiding. Hiding is actually dumb when you're going for invisible. People notice hiding. No one notices me.

7

SPECTACULARLY WEIRD

I sit down on the small strip of concrete by the container and shift to try to get comfortable. My new cell phone is denting my butt. I should put it in my bag, but I wondered what it would feel like to walk around with a phone in my back pocket like I see people do. It feels uncomfortable. I don't know how everybody does it.

I'm going to have to figure out something to tell Mama about lunch, because she won't like hearing I ate alone just like I did in elementary school.

When Mama handed me the cell phone the other day, she acted like she was giving me a golden TAP card—a ticket to hundreds of friends. (An actual TAP card gets you on buses and the Metro.)

My phone really is gold, and I guess if I had wanted one, I'd think it was cool. But here's the thing. When you have no one to text or call, a phone is sort of a mean gift in my opinion. But that's not how my mother thinks.

"You can connect with people," she said. Her voice was

serious even though she was smiling. I don't know why she thinks I have some secret horde of friends just waiting to text me.

My phone must've heard me thinking about it, because it starts vibrating. At school, the rule is, if a teacher sees your phone out, they'll take it away, but the odds seem pretty low that a teacher will see my phone way over on the far side of the field, so I risk pulling it out.

I have a message. It's from Malcolm.

Kick major booty

My brother is quite the motivational speaker.

"I thought we couldn't use our phones at school."

I jump, and my phone pops right out of my hand and onto the ground. Now it's all dirty. I wipe it off and stare up at hair so red it's like a plate of ripe strawberries. I don't know how Red Hair saw me way over here, or why he came over, so I don't say anything.

"I've been looking for you." He plops down next to me and takes out a sandwich.

"Why?" I shove my phone into my bag and pull out my own lunch. Today I went with Gruyère cheese, crackers, and a sliced Fuji apple. I'm very particular about what I eat for lunch. Mama says it seems more like I'm going wine tasting than to school, but at least she goes ahead and buys what I put on the grocery list.

"Why what?"

"Why were you looking for me?" People trying to find me isn't something I'm used to.

"I wanted to ask you about the Danish thing! I thought for sure you were into Astrid Dane because of your bag."

"I am, but I'm not a *Danish*."

It takes a second for him to process that. "Oh, I get it. It is sort of quack, I guess."

"Quack?"

"Yeah, you guys don't say that here? It's like . . . um, dumb?" The way Red Hair says it, it's like he's not sure what the word means himself.

"I've never heard anybody say that," I say. I don't add that maybe lots of people do and I just don't know. "Anyway, I don't know if it's, um, *quack*, but it's weird, since Astrid likes doughnuts. Have you ever seen her eat a *Danish*?"

"But her last name is Dane."

Yeah, *thanks*. "I know, but still."

Red Hair shrugs. "Whatever. It's just cool you like her too. In Chicago it was like no one had even heard of her! I was hoping when we moved here it would be different. And then wham! In my very first class, sitting right next to me! There you were with your bag!"

I can't help notice Red Hair uses a *lot* of exclamation marks when he talks. And he's loud. Too loud.

"Hey! You haven't asked me what my name is," he says.

I stare at him with my mouth full of the perfect blend of apple, cheese, and cracker, and wait.

"Aubrey," he says. He holds out his hand for me to shake,

which is a spectacularly weird thing to do, but I go ahead and shake his hand.

"Pleased to meet you," I lie.

"So, what's the deal here? Like, are people sway? Do they hassle you? Are they big into sports or like doing plays or something? Is there a debate team?" Aubrey's voice gets louder with each question.

I don't want to admit I haven't heard anyone use the word *sway* before, and besides, I'm pretty sure I know what it means. I shrug. "People are sway, I guess. But I don't know. I mean, it's my first day too."

"Yeah, but you're from here, right? I'm from Chicago! It's nothing like Los Angeles. It gets a whole lot colder there, first off, and it's way louder! When I found out we were moving here, I thought we'd be near the beach." He looks around as if waves might start crashing over our heads.

I see a way out. "You know, if you want to know all about Los Angeles and what people are like, you should probably find someone else. I'm not the best person to be, um, a tour guide."

"Why not? Hey, why are you eating way over here anyway?"

I swallow a sigh down with a chunk of cheese. If there is a good, acceptable answer to either of those questions, I don't have a clue what it could be. For the first time ever, I feel like maybe instead of being different, I'm strange. And I don't like this Aubrey person at all for making me feel like this.

8

THE OPPOSITE OF ME

Aubrey is still waiting for me to answer him, and so finally I just say, "I like to be left alone." *I especially like to be left alone by people who make me feel bad.*

Aubrey nods. "Yeah, I get it."

He clearly *doesn't* get it or he would leave.

In elementary school, we could eat only in the multi-purpose room, or at the tables right outside it, but in junior high, I guess they trust us a little more and you can eat wherever you want as long as you stay on campus. I wish Aubrey wanted to eat somewhere else, because the behind-the-container spot is mine.

But at least he doesn't ask me any more questions, and we eat our lunches in silence. Aubrey keeps looking like he wants to say something, but then he just takes another bite of sandwich.

When lunch is over, there's no way to avoid walking with him back toward the classrooms. The grass crunches under our feet, and I want to run and feel the sunshiny air press against my cheeks and make my ponytail fly out behind me, but I don't want to look like a freak.

I wonder if Red Hair, I mean Aubrey, toured the campus before the first day too, because he seems to know exactly where he's going, and where he's going seems to be where *I'm* going.

Figures we'd have another class together. Gee tells me how God likes to make your life more interesting by throwing the unexpected at you. Thanks, God.

I start concentrating hard as soon as we walk into English, without even thinking about what I'm doing. I focus so hard, I'm not sure if I blasted Cleo McNamara or Aubrey, but Cleo takes the desk next to mine before Aubrey can, looking a little confused at herself. I hide my smile, glad that since there's no empty seats next to me now, Aubrey has to take a seat farther back. I can't keep blasting thoughts like an out-of-control geyser, but I really couldn't have Aubrey next to me in another class.

He's too bright and loud. Basically, the opposite of me.

I'm so relieved not to be sitting next to him that I miss most of what our teacher, Mr. Humphries, says, but I do catch one scary word.

"All right, let's go!" Mr. Humphries claps his hands. "Introductory speeches."

A speech? As in, stand in front of the class and talk right out loud? Nope. That is not happening.

9
ONE INTERESTING FACT

My stress sweat goes into overdrive. There's something wrong with my lungs, because I can't breathe. And it's affecting my heart because it's beating way too fast. I don't do speeches. I have done alternate projects; I have shown up unprepared as if I forgot; I have simply refused. I've never faked being sick like other kids might have, because Mama has always said if I tried that she would "tan my hide," and although I'm not sure if she really would give me a walloping, I've never wanted to find out.

"Try to share at least one interesting fact about yourself. Maybe something no one knows or would guess about you. Like maybe you have breakfast for dinner every night, or sleep with a night-light, or write fantastic adventure stories." Mr. Humphries smiles like he's presenting us with a nice gift. He picks up a foam ball off his desk. "I'll toss this ball to someone and they'll start. Then they get to toss the ball to someone else."

I think I'm going to throw up. Actually, that's probably a great idea. If I puke all over my desk, I will not have to stand in front of the class and talk about myself. Mr. Humphries's lips are still moving, but with all the pressure building up in my ears, I can't hear a word. My head is a balloon that someone keeps blowing into even though it's already too big and about to burst.

Mr. Humphries tosses the ball to Cleo, which is way too close to tossing it to me. "You're up!" he shouts, and laughs. "You have two minutes and then toss the ball to someone else. And don't mumble. I want you to project." He steps to the side and checks his watch.

Cleo heads to the front of the room and starts talking. She doesn't look nervous at all. She pulls her curly blond hair over her shoulder and tells us about her sick cat, Chester, and how he probably won't live too much longer but that he's already lived longer than her and how if she's not at school one day soon we should know that she is probably at the vet with him, because it's his time to go.

The only reason her voice gets through the pounding in my ears is because she is projecting like nobody's business. Chester is her best friend, but she is sure he will be okay with her getting a new kitten once he is gone. I decide I don't like Cleo very much.

She throws the ball to another girl, and one by one everyone takes a turn telling us fun facts about themselves, and I start to calm down because I remember an important fact: I am invisible. No one is going to throw the ball to me because they won't notice me at all.

My breathing goes back to normal, and my heart thumpity-thumps in a nice even rhythm. I'm actually enjoying hearing about growing super-huge pumpkins and piano recitals and volleyball teams and eating the biggest brownie in the universe . . . and then Stuart Lee throws the ball to Aubrey. The one person who is sure to see me.

And suddenly I have to pee super bad. Like pee-your-pants bad, and I wave my hand like a helicopter blade, and almost before Mr. Humphries can call on me, I'm out the door and charging down the hall.

I make it. Barely.

After I finish, I wash my hands humming "Row, Row, Your Boat," like you're supposed to—or maybe that's for brushing your teeth. And then I smooth my hair and wipe my fingers along my eyebrows to make sure the hairs keep going in the same direction. Then I wash my hands again.

Then I slowly, and I mean *slow*ly, walk back to class.

Aubrey is still talking. This can't be possible. Mr. Humphries clearly said two minutes. It must've been over ten minutes. First off, how could anyone have that much to say about themselves, and second, why hasn't Mr. Humphries stopped him and gone on to the next thing on the agenda?

The way everyone looks at me as I walk to my desk tells me three things:

1) I am not invisible.

2) Aubrey was going to talk until I got back.

3) Mr. Humphries thought that was a perfectly okay thing.

Aubrey is saying something about bald people, and maybe it is supposed to be funny because he laughs, but no one else in the class does.

As soon as my butt hits my chair, Aubrey says, "And that's enough about Aubrey Banks." He throws the ball at me, and I've played catch way too many times with Malcolm for my hands not to flash up and catch it.

The ball is soft enough for me to sink my nails into, and I'm glad it is foam, because maybe it will soak up all the sweat pouring down my arms. I get up on shaky legs and glare at Aubrey as he passes by me to take his seat.

When I face the class, all I can see is the shining bright redness of Aubrey's hair. But everything else is black. I am trying to think if there is anything I can say other than my name. Can I even say my name? I open my mouth and force sounds out. Ugly sounds. Gaspy, shaky sounds. Maybe a word or two. I'm not sure. I keep blinking to try and clear the dark haze covering everything, but it's no use. I close my mouth in a hard, firm line and turn my head toward where I believe Mr. Humphries is standing.

"Thank you, Jenae," he says. His voice is soft but somehow pierces through the thick sludge surrounding me.

My vision clears, and I splash through the puddle of sweat on the floor and head back to my seat. I don't look at anyone. I most definitely do not look at the red bush nodding up and down. If Aubrey thinks he was being my friend by throwing the ball my way, he was dead wrong, and I am not interested in talking to him ever again.

"I like to start with an easy speech on the first day, just to get the jitters out," Mr. Humphries says. "We'll be reading some great books in this class, and doing a lot of writing, but we'll also learn about communication and different kinds of speeches, and you'll have an opportunity to deliver different kinds through the course of the year. By the end of the seventh grade, you'll be pros." He winks at us. "Our next one won't be impromptu like the one today. You'll have time to think about it. I'll assign it later this week."

No way can I stay in this class.

10

COMPLICATED EQUATIONS

Luckily, my last class of the day is math, and I allow the logic of complicated equations to soothe me. When the bell rings at the end of the period, I'm a little startled to realize I've survived my first day of junior high.

The walk home from John Wayne is longer than from Hancock Elementary, but I can't say I'm mad about it. Maybe I'll mind when the weather gets cooler and rainy, but today the sun is shining and my bag is swinging, and I feel grown.

I'm so busy feeling proud of myself that I don't notice the girl in front of me until I bang into her.

"Jenae!" she says, smiling.

Roxane Samuels. Malcolm's ex.

"Oh, hi, Rox," I say, feeling uncomfortable. Malcolm and Rox dated their whole senior year, and I was sad when they stopped going out, because nobody could make Malcolm laugh like Rox could. She even made Mama laugh. I don't know why her and Malcolm broke up, but afterward, Malcolm said she posted stuff online about him, and that's not a cool thing to do, so I feel like I should be angry with her on his behalf.

"I heard your brother's back home," she says, and her voice squeaks like she's trying too hard to sound casual. "How's he doing?"

"Fine," I say, because I know that's what Malcolm would want me to tell her.

Rox looks like a movie star. She's tall with dark, dark skin that is so smooth it looks painted on. And she has the biggest brown eyes I've ever seen, with long eyelashes that probably don't even need mascara. And the prettiest thing is her smile. But she's not smiling now. Rox twists the strap of her purse, and she looks sad.

"It must be hard," she says. "Basketball was . . ." Her eyes look at something far away.

"Yeah." I know what she means without her saying it, and I shrug like it doesn't matter, like Malcolm losing basketball is no big deal. And it feels awful. "But he's fine," I insist, even though I'm sure Rox knows I'm lying. Mama thought Rox was "good" for Malcolm; I just liked how relaxed Malcolm got with her, and how happy. Still, she shouldn't have put their business online.

"I should be mad at you," she says, and my eyes go wide like someone pinched me. Is she reading my mind?

"Introducing me to that Astrid Dane," she goes on, and laughs. "I'm as bad as you used to be, always waiting for a new episode."

I can't help grinning at that. "Sorry," I say.

"Your brother won't ever admit it, but I think he likes her too," she says conspiratorially.

"He sure doesn't act like it," I say, but then I want to bite my tongue. It seems wrong chatting with Rox about Malcolm, even if we're just joking around.

She smiles at me, and that makes me feel worse. "Tell you what," she says. "You got a phone?"

When I nod, she holds her hand out and I give her my phone. She types something in.

"Now you have my number. I changed it from before. Didn't need a bunch of folks from high school keeping in touch, you know?"

I don't, but I nod again anyway.

"Tell Malcolm I said hey. And if he wants to . . . reconnect, um, he can call or text me. I mean, I would be okay with that." She looks down at the ground for a minute before glancing back up at me with a shy smile. Then with a little wave, she starts to walk past me. "Bye, Jenae," she says, her voice light and airy as a spring breeze.

I continue down the street feeling guilty, even though I didn't do anything wrong. I have to fix Malcolm, not make him worse. I definitely won't be telling him I talked to his ex.

11
THE WORST THING

When I get home, Malcolm is in the big comfy chair that is usually reserved for Gee, gripping a game controller tight. He's only been gone a day, but I already miss Gee.

"What are you doing?" I ask Malcolm, as if it's not obvious.

Malcolm clicks off his game and sets down the controller. "A whole lot of nothing," he says. He stretches in that way you do when you haven't moved for a long time, and his body creaks and pops as if he's really an old man. "How was school? First day and all."

I think of the number in my phone, and a fresh wave of guilt washes over me. "It was okay." I plop down on the couch. "I didn't get lost once."

"Of course you didn't. Not after having such an excellent tour guide." He adjusts the straps of his knee brace.

I try to think of something else to say.

Before Malcolm went away to college, when we were both home from school, we'd talk outside, with Malcolm practicing his shots and me chasing down the ball for him. Mama wouldn't get home from work until close to dinnertime, and Gee was usually running the streets somewhere, so it would be just me and Malcolm. Boys' varsity always practiced late, so he didn't have to go back up to school until after dinner. I wish we were outside now. It's easier to talk when you're doing something else.

"There were people outside of school this morning. Mama got a flier. About the school's name?" Mama didn't seem very concerned about it, but at least it's something to say. Malcolm must not have heard anything about it, because he just shrugs; then he winces and rubs his leg.

I start gnawing on my lip. I hate seeing him in pain.

"So what was the worst thing?" he asks.

I'm not sure when Malcolm and I started doing this. Mama had read in a book or magazine or something that over dinner we should tell each other the best thing that happened to us that day. Do you know how hard it is to come up with good things every day? Almost impossible. Malcolm and I would say things like *A bird didn't poop on my head. I didn't get detention.* Eventually Mama got tired of the whole thing and let us stop, but Malcolm and I realized coming up with something bad that happened was super easy.

It might sound like it would be depressing to think of the worst thing, but actually, it makes whatever that worst thing is seem not so bad. I mean, if the worst thing you can say about your day is that you tripped on some stairs, it's not so hard to see how it actually wasn't that bad and could've been a whole lot worse.

Today my worst thing is pretty bad, though. "I had to give a speech." Just thinking about it makes a nasty taste climb up my throat.

Malcolm laughs. "Is that all?"

"I don't like talking in front of people." This is what is called an understatement. To make my point I add, "I thought I was going to die. Like, seriously, drop dead right there in class."

"And yet, here you sit."

I pull at a thread on my jeans. "I guess."

"Are you or are you not still alive? Huh? Is this a zombie sitting up here in my house? Are you about to try and eat my face?"

"Shut up, Malcolm." I can't help giggling. And because he's made me feel like the worst possible thing is almost funny, I mess everything up. "So, what's your worst thing today?" As soon as I ask, I want to gobble the words out of the air. I already know what his worst thing is. What it is every day since his injury.

Proving my point, Malcolm doesn't even answer me. Instead he reaches for his game controller and restarts his game. "You should probably get going on your homework."

"Malcolm," I say, just as if I know what words are going to follow.

"What?" he asks, but doesn't set down his controller.

"I didn't know how much I was going to miss you when you left."

"Well, I'm back now, aren't I?"

I have to gulp at that. "Malcolm, do you believe that we can make things happen? Just by wanting them super bad?"

Now he does put the controller back down and looks at me as if I have completely lost it. "What do you think, Jenae?"

I *have* lost it. All he wants is to play basketball again. I bet he doesn't think it's going to happen just by wanting it really bad. And I don't know why I'm punishing myself like this, but I can't help it. "Was it everything you wanted? Playing college ball?" My question comes out as a shaky whisper.

"No," Malcolm says. He shifts around in the chair like he's trying to find a comfortable way to sit. "It was hard. Like really, really hard. The books there? No joke. Studying and practicing twenty-four seven was the hardest thing I've ever done. And if someone had asked me if I wanted a break? Just a second to catch my breath, right? I might've said yes." Malcolm stares down at his knee. "But not like this. No way. It was hard, but it was . . . where I was supposed to be." His voice is low and sad.

"Well, you still have us. No matter what. And maybe you can do something else," I say, hoping to brighten his mood.

"I *know*." Malcolm shakes his head at me. "But you don't get it. Ball was what I had for *me*. It was my *future*. Don't be coming at me saying I can just pick something else like I'm standing at a damn apple tree."

I want to argue with him but don't know how. When I don't say anything, he goes back to playing his game. Slowly, I get up and start my way upstairs.

I have to fix him. I *have* to.

12

A NEW CONTACT

Each step, I try to think of something, anything I can do to help Malcolm. *You break it, you buy it* rattles around in my head. But how are you supposed to fix a broken person? When I get to the top of the stairs, I think of Rox's number hiding in my phone. And I think of how she used to make Malcolm laugh so hard he couldn't breathe. Maybe if I were to tell him about seeing Rox, it would make Malcolm smile. Or maybe it would make him really mad. But something has to make him see that his life isn't over even if it turns out he can't play basketball anymore. And maybe Rox could be the one to do it.

Once I get to my room, I pull out my phone. I stare at Rox's number and wonder if there's something I could text her that could end up helping Malcolm.

If I were Astrid Dane, I could probably figure this out. Each show, she's set on solving a problem, and so far, the only mysteries Astrid can't solve are how she ended up being immortal and why she has all those ghosts inside her.

My thumb hovers over Rox's name. I can't fix Malcolm's

knee, but if I can change the way he feels about being back home, maybe I won't be the worst sister ever.

Before I have time to change my mind, I text:

My brother was really glad to hear I saw you.

Then I press send.

It makes me feel a little brave even though I just texted a complete lie. But it feels like something Astrid Dane would do. I bet if Astrid and I met in real life, we'd be friends. I click on the little plus sign to add a new contact and put Astrid in the first-name space, and then, before I can worry about how weird I must be to do this, I put Dane in the last-name space. Then I put some random numbers in for her phone number.

Seeing Astrid's name like she's a friend I could call makes me smile, even though it probably makes me the oddest person alive.

A few minutes later my phone buzzes with a message from Rox. It's just a smiling face, but it's a start.

13

QUESTION EIGHT

By the time Mama gets home from work, I have started the sauce for the noodles and am cutting up lots of lettuce for a salad.

"Where's your brother?" is the first question out of Mama's mouth.

I'm not bothered she asks about Malcolm before me. He's the one who's hurting right now.

"Upstairs," I say, not looking up from the cutting board.

She sighs and slides out of her shoes. "What's for dinner?"

"Spaghetti and a green salad. We're out of bread, so I'm not making garlic bread." And because the broiler scares me. Once, I reached in to pull a tray out of the oven when the broiler was on and I forgot to put on an oven mitt. Even though my fingers only touched the top rack for a second, it still hurt really bad. Mama had me hold my fingers under cold water while Gee ran outside and broke off a piece of aloe vera from a plant on the porch. He smeared the gooey guts over my fingers, but the tips of my fingers still hurt for over a week.

"Make sure you add bread to the shopping list, okay?"

Does that count as a question? I think so.

"You're not putting anything weird in the sauce, are you?"

I like experimenting in the kitchen, but Mama doesn't want anything fancy. Last time I made spaghetti, I sliced up anchovies and garlic-filled olives and added them into the sauce, and Mama spit her first mouthful right out.

"No, Mama," I say. "It's plain, boring spaghetti."

"Am I hearing a tone?"

"No."

Mama pads over to me and takes a few shreds of lettuce and dribbles them into her mouth. "No tomatoes?"

"We're out."

"No tomatoes, no bread. Why didn't you ask Malcolm to take you to the market?"

"I didn't want to bother him."

That's seven questions already and not one of them has been about my first day of school.

Mama looks up at the ceiling, and I bet she's wondering about going upstairs and giving Malcolm a talking-to.

She must decide against it, because she returns her attention to me. "How was school?"

Question eight. "Fine. Some of the teachers talked about the name change. I guess it's going to be decided soon."

"Mm" is all Mama says to that. Maybe she doesn't care what my school is called. Then she starts tapping her foot, but without her heels on, it's just soft smooshes against tile, not crisp, angry snaps. "How were *folks*, Jenae? Anyone talk to you? You talk to anybody?"

"Everyone seems nice." Then I add, "I talked to a boy. He—"

Before I can explain, Mama says, "A *boy*?" She sounds suspicious.

"Not like that, Mama. We just talked in class. . . ." I shut my mouth because I was going to say we had lunch together, but that seems like saying way too much.

"Guess I should be happy you talked to somebody," Mama mumbles.

Her phone buzzes, and when she pulls it out, I realize now's my chance to talk to her about getting out of my English class.

"Mama," I start. Sometimes my mouth begins talking before my brain has totally figured out what I want to say. "Our English teacher is making us do speeches."

"What's the matter with that?" she asks, but she's tapping out a message, so I know she's only partway listening.

"I think I should get into a different English class. One that focuses on writing, like English is supposed to."

"Hmmm."

I can't tell if Mama is hmming something on her phone or me. "Will you write a note to the school?"

Mama sets down her phone.

Uh-oh.

"Jenae."

"Yes?"

"What's really going on?"

I can feel sweat sprouting. "I should have the *better* English teacher, and instead I got stuck with Mr. Humphries. If you tell them I should be in Ms. Garcia's class, they'll have to switch me."

"Is that boy you were talking to in Ms. Garcia's class?" Mama asks. "Is that why you really want to switch?"

"No! We're in the same class now. It doesn't have anything to do with him."

"Wait a minute. You want me to get you out of a class that has the one person at the school you actually talked to? Now you know that's not going to happen." Mama goes back to her phone, her judgment served, but then she adds one last dig. "Besides, Mr. Humphries is the best English teacher they got at that school. And he's Black? Girl, stop playing."

Shoot. I should've known Mama already knew all about Mr. Humphries.

14

THE UNINVITED

When Mama drops me off at school the next day, I see the people with fliers again, but there seem to be more of them. I scurry past the crowd, not wanting any of them to try and talk to me.

I'm surprised when I get to first period—Aubrey is waiting outside the class—and even more surprised when I realize he's waiting for me.

"Hi, Jenae!" he says, with so much enthusiasm I almost turn around to see if there is another Jenae behind me. "I've been waiting forever for you!"

"Uh, hi," I say, but I don't stop to talk. I just keep walking into the class, and he follows close behind me, and he keeps yipping and yapping, talking about Astrid Dane and how cool she is and how great our bags are and whether I've seen every single episode and read every single graphic novel.

People who are already in their seats look at him like he's from a different planet. Actually, they are looking at both of us that way. That's not fair. Even I know you're not supposed to act like a caffeinated puppy dog at school. I rush to my seat, trying to make it clear I'm not really with him, but he sticks to me like duct tape.

When I sit down, Geoffrey shifts in his seat as if to put as much distance as possible between me and Aubrey.

I don't like loud. Being loud gets you seen.

I could never be friends with someone like Aubrey.

Unfortunately, Aubrey doesn't seem to understand this fact, because even though I ignored him in history and hustled out of class without stopping to talk, he still shows up at my lunch spot again.

"Hey," I say, with not much enthusiasm, staring at his fiery-red hair. Why would anyone choose such a loud color?

"Hi! I woke up late today and didn't have time to make a good lunch! Just two-day-old chicken and rice, but my mom is a really good cook, so it's good, right? Just not all that *school-*friendly." All while he's talking, he sits down, takes out his container of chicken and rice, shows it to me, takes out a fork. Then he shovels in a mouthful of food and chews and stares at me, waiting for me to say something, I guess.

It's not as if I've never had a friend in my entire life. From, like, kindergarten all the way through second grade, the girls at school hung together in a big clump. I guess we were friends? We played hopscotch together, and then two square and tetherball. If you didn't want to play, you still hung around the people who did. But then Emory Cooper had a birthday party and she only invited five girls. And suddenly, we weren't all one big group anymore. There were the girls who had gotten invited and the

47

ones who hadn't. I didn't mind not getting invited, because it was a horse-riding party and I'm scared of horses. But other girls felt bad and left out. And they didn't like that I *didn't* feel bad. And so I didn't fit in with the invited or the uninvited. And the next birthday party (Shondra Welch's), she only invited the girls who didn't get invited to Emory's, but she didn't invite me either.

From then on, there were the popular girls, the regular girls, and me. It was sort of a relief. I didn't like the recess games. I didn't like running around and getting sweaty. I really just wanted to sit in the library and read, and so that's what I started doing, and the only person I think was bothered by any of it was Mama. You'd think she would've been happy she didn't have to drop me off for playdates or anything anymore, but instead she would poke and poke, asking me, "What happened to so-and-so?" I never had a good answer, and eventually she stopped asking, but I overheard her on the phone talking to one of her sisters saying how strange it was that I didn't hang out with anyone. How *odd* it seemed. I wanted to tell Mama right then that I was okay being odd. It just means being different from what is expected, and what's wrong with that?

"You know," I say to Aubrey, "it's fine with me if you want to sit somewhere else." I don't want him to think he's stuck sitting with me just because he ended up here yesterday.

Aubrey looks around, glances across the field at the large lunch table area. "You want to go over there?"

I shake my head. "No, I meant . . ." But I don't finish because there doesn't seem to be a way to finish that sentence without making things awkward. I decide to talk about something else. "What's Chicago like?"

Aubrey tells me about a museum with a huge dinosaur skeleton, and the train that's like a subway but is aboveground, and a lake so big it's like an ocean, and winters so cold it freezes the snot to your face.

"So *none* of your friends like Astrid Dane?" I cut him off to ask.

Aubrey's face gets weird. Uncomfortable. Like I asked him something too personal.

But then he smiles. "Nah, they weren't into stuff like that." He shovels some chicken into his mouth and then gulps it down. "That's why it was so sway meeting you!"

"What's sway?" I ask, even though I think I know.

Aubrey rocks back and forth and gets a goofy look on his face. "It's good. It's going with the flow. You know? Sway!"

How can I not smile?

I get worried on the way to English, but today, Mr. Humphries sticks to normal stuff and doesn't mention speeches at all. He talks about the book we're going to read. *Coraline.* It sounds creepy, and I can't wait to start it. If Mr. Humphries would just stick to reading and writing, I think I'd love his class.

As we file out for sixth period, Aubrey lets his bag hit mine. "See ya later!"

"Y-yeah," I say, stuttering a little, which is dumb, but I don't know what to do with all of Aubrey's enthusiasm. It's too much.

Maya Cruz gives me a small smile as she passes me, and I wonder if she's thinking how strange it is that someone is talking to me. Maya's nice, but she was one of the girls who got invited to Emory's party, and I'm not used to her smiling at me.

When I get out of sixth period and start to head home, I find out by *later*, Aubrey didn't mean tomorrow, he meant after school, because I hear him hollering my name even though I'm already halfway down the street. Everyone turns to stare, and I freeze. That makes it really easy for him to catch up to me.

"What?" I demand, my voice low and angry. "*What* do you want?" All the good feeling I had toward Aubrey evaporates like hot breath fogging up glass.

Aubrey's smile takes the smallest dip. "J-j-just saying hi! Are you going home?"

"You can't just shout at people," I say. My face feels hot. It feels like hundreds of eyes are pointed at me. "I gotta go. I'll see you *tomorrow*," I say, making it clear that our conversation is over. Then I turn away and start walking down the street again, keeping my head down and holding my bag tight against my side. I don't relax until I get two blocks away.

15

RED VINES

That puts me right in front of the store that sells my favorite candy, and I figure I deserve something sweet.

I head straight for the candy aisle, hoping there will be a package of Red Vines. Sometimes there's only black licorice, and no way am I eating a mouthful of bitter yuck. Other times they only have the Twizzlers brand, and that's like eating a bunch of sticky wax. But the blue-and-white-striped box is right there, filled with fat red straws of yum.

The only thing better than walking in the sunshine and eating Red Vines is watching Astrid Dane while eating Red Vines.

As I turn the corner of our block, already thinking how I can probably manage at least a few episodes of Astrid Dane before Mama gets home, a voice beckons to me.

"Hola, Jenae!"

A big, wide smile busts out all over my face. "Tía Rosalie!"

Tía Rosalie lives a few houses down from us, and even though she's not my aunt, I've called her Tía for as long as I can remember. Malcolm does too. I think everyone in the neighborhood does.

She sets her garden hose on the grass and comes down her walkway, rolling her hips like she's about ready to dance. She says big women are the ones who really know how to move, and I guess she's right, because she sure can shake it.

"Your favorite hasn't changed, eh, Jenae?" she asks, nodding at my candy. She takes off her gardening gloves and tucks them under an arm.

"Mm-hm" is all I can manage with my mouth full of licorice.

She reaches over and flicks one of my braids. I have two today. Running down the sides of my head like a railroad. "Tell me, Jenae, how do you feel about starting junior high?"

Tía Rosalie knows everything about everyone. Mama doesn't like it one bit. "Okay, I guess," I say.

"Have you heard about the name change?" she asks.

I nod, but then I admit, "Some people were passing out fliers, but I don't really know much about it."

Tía's eyes start to sparkle. "Sylvia Mendez Junior High. That will be the new name! About time they honor *our* community."

"Our?" I ask.

"Mexican," Tía Rosalie says proudly, pointing a thumb at herself. Then she adds, "Puerto Rican too, of course, because Sylvia Mendez was both, but even for the Colombians and Salvadorans and Dominicans." She throws her arms wide. "There are many, many Latino cultures here, but on this, we are one."

"But," I say. I don't want to say the wrong thing. "Since it's always been John Wayne Junior High, can the name just get changed?"

Tía Rosalie nods. "The school district decides," she says. "There will be a board meeting soon, and then we'll get the new name." She sounds as if she already knows what's going to happen. "I'll be so happy when they change it! I've been telling my grandkids all about it. Violeta will start there next year."

"Gee is gonna be mad," I say quietly.

"How is Grady?" Tía asks. "In Vegas, no?"

"Yep," I say. This is the type of thing Mama complains about. She doesn't know how Tía Rosalie can know the things she knows. Mama thinks Tía spies on everyone, but since she spends most of her time out front gardening, she probably just sees and hears all the goings-on.

"Ach, such a rolling stone, that man. I am praying for him," she says. Then she blows me a kiss to send me on my way.

At home, I ask Malcolm why Tía Rosalie would be praying for Gee.

"You know Tía," he says. "Always praying for somebody."

I wonder if she's praying for Malcolm.

"Malcolm, would you care if they changed the name of the school?" All of his basketball trophies from his junior high team say John Wayne on them.

"Nope," he says. "Doesn't make any difference to me."

"But . . ." I want to say if the name changes, it would be

like me and Malcolm went to different schools, but I know how silly that would sound. But the truth is, I like following behind him.

"It's the same school, Jenae. What do you care what it's called?" He sounds annoyed now, and I know I need to leave him alone. I wish he wasn't so grumpy all the time.

Before I start my homework, I take out my phone and try to think of something else I can text Rox. After rejecting all sorts of dumb ideas, I finally type:

How can I get Malcolm to laugh?

I think it's pretty clever, because I don't actually say he's *not* laughing, but Rox is smart enough to read between the lines.

Rox doesn't answer right away, but eventually she does.

Have him watch old episodes of Martin.

I nod as I read her text. She definitely knows my brother. She's going to help me fix him.

16

AN ORIGIN STORY

The next day, when I get to school, I'm not so surprised to see Aubrey waiting for me outside of history.

"What does your mom do?" he asks.

It's a strange way to say hello. Even *I* know how to say hello and goodbye better than Aubrey.

"She's a marketing director." I shrug after saying it, as if I know what that means.

Aubrey nods like *he* knows what it means. "My mom just got a job in a restaurant. In Chicago she did people's taxes from home, but she was always practicing her cooking and watching those chef-competition shows."

"That's . . ." I stop because I don't know what it is. Aubrey waits for me to finish my sentence. "Interesting." It's all I can think of.

"Not really. But her food is."

I slide past Aubrey into history, and of course he trails right behind me.

All through class I try to think of something to say so Aubrey won't hunt me down at lunch. It's not that I don't *like* him, but if he's trying to make friends, I'm not the best person to start off with. I remember he asked about acting and sports, so as soon as class is over, I tell him, "Some guys back in elementary school played tag football on the field at lunch. I bet they do that here."

"I'm not really into football."

"Oh. Um, well, they probably play pickup basketball games over—"

"Naw," he cuts me off. "I'm not that into that."

"Okay. There's probably like a drama club or something that maybe meets at lunch."

"Drama isn't my thing. But boy, if there's a debate team? *That* I would be all over."

"Debate?" The only thing I know about debating is when there's an election and Mama and Gee will watch the candidates debate the issues. It's super boring.

"Yeah! I was really into that in Chicago. We went to competitions and stuff."

"Oh, um . . ." I try to remember the word Aubrey used. "That's swack."

Aubrey's mouth pinches like he's trying to hold back a laugh, so I'm pretty sure I've gotten the word wrong, but he doesn't say anything, just looks at me. I want to ask him what he sees when he looks at me, but that would be a really dumb thing to ask, so I don't. He stares so long, I think maybe I accidentally disappeared.

A girl from elementary, Beth Hashimoto, bumps into me

with her backpack, like I'm not even there, making me stumble forward.

Aubrey puts his arm up to brace me so I don't fall.

Beth adjusts her backpack, and I think for a second she might say sorry, or hi, or to watch out, but she just fixes her hair behind her ears, looks right through me, and continues down the hall. I watch her for a moment and then realize Aubrey is still staring at me.

I'm going to be late to my next class, but it seems wrong to walk away without either of us saying anything, so finally I say, "What?"

He gets that big old grin of his, making even his eyes look like they're laughing. "Hah! Made you talk! And it's *sway*!"

This boy is a goofball with a capital G. And shaking my head, I march off to class.

It's not until I'm sitting in my next class that I realize I didn't make sure he sits with someone else at lunch instead of me.

So of course he shows up in my spot again. I probably should've sat somewhere else, but this is a good spot, and it's mine, and I did sort of wonder if he'd come over even after I gave him some hints on where else he could sit.

And as soon as he settles in with his lunch, he starts up with questions.

"What do you think the deal is with Astrid's ghosts? Like how many are there, and where do they come from?" he asks. "Do you think she's secretly a vampire and the ghosts are people she drained?"

"Oh, I never thought of that. Maybe *that's* why she's immortal! That would be so cool if she was a vampire!" I shove grapes into my mouth to keep more words from coming out. I almost used as many exclamation points as Aubrey, and that is not how I like to talk.

"We should write an origin story. You can write it, and I'll do the drawings!"

I'm shocked by Aubrey's suggestion. It seems like such a . . . friend thing to do together, and we aren't friends.

"Maybe," I say.

On the way to English, Aubrey talks so loud that people turn to look at us and I want to disappear. I don't understand why his volume is always set so high.

Mr. Humphries starts talking about themes in the books we'll be reading and how friendship is a common one. Aubrey says right out loud, "Like us, right, Jenae?" and my cheeks burn with embarrassment.

Maybe he loves attention, but I sure don't, and so once I'm done with sixth period, I hustle out of class and jam down the street, because I don't want a repeat of yesterday with Aubrey calling my name and throwing all sorts of attention my way. My shoulders are up near my ears, and I keep expecting to hear him yelling, but thankfully, he doesn't.

When I get home, Malcolm is on the couch attached to his knee-bender machine. It's not really called that, but that's what it does. It moves his leg slowly up and down, bending his knee over and over. I hate seeing him using it, like he can't move his leg by himself.

He has earbuds in and is bobbing his head to a song, so I just wave at him. He gives me a half smile, and I head to my room.

Before I start homework, I take out my phone and look at Astrid Dane's number. I wish I could really call her. On the show, Astrid has a cell phone but she never calls anybody, she just uses it to google stuff and take selfies. She's sort of addicted to selfies.

I hold my phone out and take a selfie. My first one. The vest I made is hanging in my closet. I grab it and put it on, then sling my clock bag over my shoulder and take some more, acting like I'm cool like Astrid, and that's when my door opens.

"Dude," Malcolm says, "you are *seriously* tripping."

Right behind Malcolm is Aubrey.

No way. No way is this flaming-hot-Cheeto-hair boy up here in my room.

"What are you doing here?" I ask, letting my bag slide off my shoulder and onto the floor. "How do you know where I live?"

Aubrey's so fair, it's easy to see the blush exploding all over his face like a bucket of red paint got tipped over his head. It makes his freckles stand out even more. "I sort of . . . followed you?" He glances over at Malcolm, and I'm sure Aubrey's thinking that following a girl home is at the top of things her big brother might beat him up for.

He *followed* me? That's creepy. I look over at Malcolm, and right at that moment, I wouldn't mind if Malcolm *did* beat Aubrey up. Not one bit.

Malcolm's eyes go cold, and he looks back and forth between me and Aubrey. "Hold up, you *do* know this dude, right?" Malcolm asks me, and I only hesitate a second before nodding.

"He's cool?" Malcolm asks, and at first I don't answer, because I don't know if Aubrey is cool or not, but with a sigh, I nod again.

"All right, then," Malcolm says. He turns to Aubrey. "'Cause following a girl home, dude? Following *anybody* home? Not cool. Not cool at all. You hear me? That's some creeper mess. Haven't you heard of Me Too?"

Aubrey nods fast, his eyes going extra wide. "It wasn't like that. I swear!"

Malcolm looks at me again, and I give him a little smile, letting him know I'm okay. "Cool." He turns and crutches away. "Leave your door open," he throws over his shoulder, and my cheeks burn.

As soon as Malcolm is out of earshot, Aubrey starts talking really fast at me. "I wasn't following at first! You were just going the same way I was going, and it was sort of fun once I knew you didn't know I was behind you."

I stare stonily at him, and his smile slips a little.

"I was being a spy, you know? Like Astrid?"

If he thought mentioning Astrid Dane was going to make me think this was okay, he's absolutely wrong. "You can't just follow people."

"I know. I'm sorry, I just . . ." Aubrey shrugs, and for a blip he really does look sorry, but then his big grin spreads across his face. "You really didn't notice?"

Maybe that's the thing that bothers me the most. I had no clue he was behind me. To be fair, I wasn't expecting to be followed, so I wasn't trying to be invisible, but that's no excuse. What if he had been a deranged person?

What if he *is* a deranged person?

17

A TOUGH ONE

"Let's go downstairs," I say. If he is dangerous, I'd rather deal with it down in the kitchen, where at least I have both the front and back door to try and get to.

Music pounds Malcolm's door, making the carpet dance. I quietly sing along to the angry words slathering the hall. Malcolm says he likes to feel music over his skin, through his hair follicles, down into his ankles and toes. He used to say it got him pumped up for a game; I don't know what it pumps him up for now.

Before he left for school, the music he listened to talked about parties and girls and being better than everyone else, but when he came back, the words got heated. Hot enough to melt everything away.

"Didn't Astrid Dane wear a vest like that in the 'Corruption' episode?" Aubrey asks as he follows me to the kitchen.

"Mm-hmm," I say, and I can't hide the grin teasing my face. He doesn't *seem* dangerous.

"Cool buttons," he says.

"Thanks." The word comes out a little breathlessly. "I actually found the buttons first, and that's when I knew I had to make the vest." I've never had someone to talk to about Astrid Dane. It feels strange, but in a good way.

Aubrey takes a step back, as if he needs some distance to get a really good look, and then he nods appreciatively. "Sway," he says. Then he holds up his hand as if I were talking and he needs me to hold on. He pulls out his phone and reads a message, then taps something back. He looks a little annoyed, which is a strange expression for him. But when he puts away his phone, he's back to being all smiles.

But I don't know what to do now. I've never had someone over. On TV shows it seems like when kids hang out, they are always snacking and joking around. I'm down for the snacking part of that. I get some crackers out from the cabinet.

"Your house is really big," Aubrey says, staring at the space next to the kitchen, what Gee calls the butler's pantry—it's just a bunch of cabinets, but it sounds fancy.

"Yeah, Gee—that's my grandfather—told me rich people used to live all up and down this street. That's why the houses are so huge."

"Are you guys rich?" Aubrey asks, his eyes wide and surprised.

"No," I say, and giggle. "Gee said a Black movie star moved onto the street, when it was only white people living here before that. And all the rich white people started moving away." I shrug. It all happened so long ago, and I can't even imagine the neighborhood not being full of all sorts of people. "After they all left, then just regular people like Gee and Nana June bought the houses." I love our house, and even though I think it's silly for someone to move so they don't have to live by a Black family, I'm sort of glad they did.

Aubrey keeps looking around and nodding, taking everything in. Then he looks up at the ceiling, as if he can see right up to the second floor. "So was that your brother?" he asks.

"Who else would it be?" I ask, knowing where this is going.

"You guys don't look much alike."

Malcolm and I don't look anything alike. The whole different-dads thing.

"I know," is all I tell Aubrey.

"Why is he on crutches?"

Because I was selfish. "He had an operation on his knee."

"He's pretty tall."

"He played basketball." I hear the *ed* tucked on the end like a bad dog's tail, and I can't take it back. I've never said it out loud before. *Played*, not *plays*. I pull the water pitcher out of the fridge and slam it so hard on the counter, the plastic cracks and water seeps out the bottom.

Aubrey grabs the broken pitcher out of my hand and dumps the rest of the water into the sink. He looks around for the recycling trash and puts the pitcher in there, then grabs paper towels and wipes the water from the counter. Anybody would think he was the one who lives here, not me.

"It's just a pitcher," he says. "No big deal, right?"

"I guess not." I want Aubrey to leave. I want to go up to my room and lie on my bed and let Malcolm's music melt me.

"I wasn't thirsty anyway," Aubrey says. "And even if I was . . ." He turns on the faucet and dips his head under it and guzzles up water like everyone knows you're not supposed to do.

"We have glasses," I say, but I can't say it without laughing.

"Hah! Made you smile," Aubrey crows, and wipes his mouth with the back of his hand.

"You make it sound like that's so hard or something."

"You're a tough one. I was thinking I might have to go to extraordinary measures."

I sort of wish I hadn't smiled, because I'm curious what *extraordinary measures* Aubrey might've tried.

"So, um . . ." I start to dig my toe into the kitchen tile. The crackers are still on the counter. Should I put them on a plate?

"What did you think of the last episode?" Aubrey's smile is smeared across his whole face, as if he's really only five. Most people my age aren't quite as wide open as he seems to be. Maybe that's how people act in Chicago.

"I thought it was cool how she sneaked onto the pirate ship," I say.

Watching Astrid Dane episodes is almost like reading those Magic Tree House books. Since she's immortal and has been around for hundreds and hundreds of years, you never know what era you'll find her in. And then you wait to see what mystery she's going to solve.

But since Astrid Dane isn't a regular TV show, it can take a superlong time before a new episode gets posted. The last one was weeks ago.

"Who's your favorite ghost?" Aubrey asks.

The question is sort of like asking what Harry Potter house you'd be in and feels personal, but it does make me curious who Aubrey's favorite ghost might be. I squint my eyes at him. Explorer. Definitely. I'm not even sure if I have a favorite, but Aubrey is looking at me expectantly. "The witch," I finally say.

"She's pretty del."

"Del?" I ask.

"Yeah!" Aubrey says. "Del!"

Aubrey acts like he can define a word by just repeating it a bunch of times.

"What does it even mean?"

"Del," he says again, like it should be obvious. Then he gets red. "It's short for delicious?"

"You think the witch is delicious?"

"No! But saying something's cool doesn't mean it's actually cold, right?"

Aubrey has turned the color of a Christmas ribbon.

"Ooookay," I say.

He starts twisting a tiny bit of his hair and then lets go, but the hair stays twisted. Just one small, tight red twist sticking from the front of his head like a tiny horn.

"What's the deal with the color of your hair?" I can tell his hair is not any kind of natural color, which means he's choosing to go around looking like a stoplight. Even a stuffed animal would be embarrassed to have hair that red.

Aubrey runs his fingers through his tight curls, destroying his little horn and making his hair poke out in different directions. "No deal."

Don't tell me, then.

"I could probably help you with giving speeches," he says. "I really like stuff like that. It's only scary the first few times. You see how easy it is to talk to me, right here? That's all you have to do when you give a speech. It's the same thing. You could practice with me."

"No, thanks," I say.

Aubrey's smile is a little shaky, but then it grows, reaching all the way up to his topaz eyes. "Yep," he says. "Tough one."

Talking about Astrid Dane is one thing, but speeches? I'd rather eat burned eggs. "Do you know your way home?" I ask, putting an end to this conversation.

Aubrey winks at me, which I didn't know was something people our age did in real life. "Gotcha!" He grabs his book bag off the floor and heads out of the kitchen, and before I know it, I hear the front door open and close.

I'm not disappointed. Not at all. I wanted him to leave. But I don't think that was a normal way to leave someone's house. Aren't you supposed to say goodbye? Saying *gotcha* isn't saying goodbye. I don't know much about Aubrey, but I have figured out one thing: he's as odd as I am.

I make my way upstairs and stand outside Malcolm's door. His music is muted, like he has a pillow over his small portable speaker. I want to ask him to help me make dinner. I want to ask him if he's okay. I want to ask him if he could try and be happy about being at home.

Instead, I go back downstairs to make dinner by myself. But before I do, I send Rox another text.

Malcolm was talking about how much fun you two used to have. He sure misses you.

Almost immediately, Rox texts me back.

I miss him too.

I tap my teeth with my fingernail, thinking. This is going good. I don't think it's too bad that I'm not telling the exact truth because I bet Malcolm does actually miss Rox.

He feels bad about how things ended. But you know Malcolm. He'll never tell you.

I stare at the message for over a minute. Maybe I'm going too far. This doesn't seem right, to be getting all into their business. But what if it helps Malcolm? I press send.

18
ALL THAT TIME

The next day, Aubrey makes himself comfortable right next to me at lunch, and I'm not all that interested in trying to get him to eat somewhere else.

"I like your lunches," he says. "It's like what my mom would eat."

Today, I packed some Brie and soft French bread and olives and a little bit of salami. I shrug. "It's not that different from a ham sandwich," I say, putting a bit of Brie on bread and then a piece of salami. I take a bite. "Totally normal."

Aubrey pulls out his (boring) sandwich and takes a huge bite. Then he says, "So why don't you like giving speeches?"

What he actually says is *"Ohh whuh dur ur eyck grring speeshes?"* But I understand him just fine.

"I don't understand why we're doing speeches in English. It's supposed to be about reading and writing and, I don't know, dangling modifiers," I say.

Aubrey's eyes go pretty wide while he's trying to get that monster bite down his throat. "But like Mr. Humphries said, not all speeches will be extemporaneous, so for those we'll have to *write* it first."

I'm not going to lie. It's sort of impressive that Aubrey can reel off a big word like that with no trouble. "Then we should just be able to hand in what we wrote."

"You mean without giving the speech?"

I nod.

"But . . . then it wouldn't be a speech."

"Exactly."

Aubrey takes a few more bites of his sandwich, and I eat one green olive, then two black ones.

Suddenly, he grins at me and snaps his fingers. "You know what? For your next speech, you should do it on Astrid Dane. You wouldn't be nervous at all. Click!"

I've never heard anyone use *click* like that, but I can sort of figure out what he means. "It's not click," I say. "It's *un*-click!"

Aubrey cracks up at that. "You're so funny! You can't say un-click! Click is like . . ." He looks around like maybe the defi-nition is lying on the grass or up in the sky. "*Click*, like . . ." He holds up his hands as if he's holding a camera and then presses down with his finger. "You know, it's such a sure thing, so obvi-ous, it's like a picture? You can see it?" He laughs some more, and him laughing at me for not using a dumb word right is annoying.

"Well, if something can be *so* obvious, then something can be so *not* obvious." I shove an olive into my mouth.

Maybe Aubrey doesn't see how annoyed I am, because he

smiles. "Yeah, okay. Un-click. I'll give you that one. But I still think I'm right. You'd give a great Astrid Dane speech."

The *thought* of standing in front of the class again with them staring at me makes me get all sweaty and anxious. My heart starts thudding hard like I just finished running a mile. There's not one thing I could do that would make me survive giving another speech. I shove the rest of my lunch back into my bag. Why did Aubrey have to ruin everything?

"You can practice it with me. I'm good at speeches. I—"

"I'M NOT GIVING ANOTHER SPEECH! JUST LEAVE ME ALONE!" I stomp away from Aubrey, and I don't stop until I march all the way to Mr. Humphries's class.

Mr. Humphries already has the door open, even though it's not time for class. Before I realize what I'm doing, I start arguing against me giving speeches. I tell him about alternative projects I could do. Or superlong papers, or extra book reports, but Mr. Humphries just smiles and says he understands, but no, I have to do a speech.

"I just don't understand why we have to do speeches in English," I say, even though I know it's no use.

Mr. Humphries laughs as if I told a great joke. "Effective communication is important, Jenae. And learning how to think about things. These speeches will teach you a lot more than just about standing in front of people." Then he says, "And by the way, that was actually a pretty good persuasive speech you delivered."

Mr. Humphries thinks he's funny. And obviously I didn't give an effective speech, since I didn't persuade him. I slink to my desk.

When class starts, Mr. Humphries announces that he got a great idea at lunch for our next speech assignment. "I'd like you to present an argument—in other words, a persuasive speech."

I feel like Mr. Humphries is making fun of me, and I slide low in my chair and steam.

After class, Aubrey heads out without looking my way, and I'm certain I don't have to worry about him bugging me anymore, so I'm really surprised when I come out of school at the end of the day and find him standing there. The way his face lights up when he sees me, it's obvious he's been waiting for me, and I know if I try to walk past him, he'll just start shouting at me.

I walk over. I have to pass through a small group of people waving signs that say things about history and Sylvia Mendez and diversity.

It is obvious the signs are supporting the school name change—which means they don't really have anything to do with me.

"Uh, sorry for yelling at you at lunch," I tell Aubrey, clenching and unclenching the strap of my messenger bag.

"That's okay," he says. He reaches up and twists a small piece of that wild redness flaming on top of his head like he did before. Round and round he twists while he looks at me, and then he asks, "Can I come over?"

Gee is forever talking to me about two roads and being

careful about which one you put your feet on. Staring down at the sidewalk, I can see the two paths clear as day. Part of me wants to tell Aubrey to bother someone else, but another part is sort of curious what it might be like to get to know him better. Maybe I can at least find out why he dyes his hair fire-engine red.

"Sure," I finally say. "I mean, okay, you can come."

As we start down the street, Aubrey pulls his phone out of his pocket. I guess he must've gotten a message. He shakes his head while reading and then types in a message and puts his phone away, but we don't get very far before he pulls his phone out again, and this time he sighs before typing another message. Then instead of putting his phone in his pocket, he drops it in his bag. I want to ask him who is sending him so many messages, but it seems nosy and none of my business.

For the rest of the walk, Aubrey talks about an Astrid Dane episode where she runs across a dark frozen lake and the ice cracks and she goes right into that freezing-cold water. No one's around, and she gets trapped. It's sort of tragic and beautiful at the same time. Her hair is swirling all around her, and even though she's underwater and freezing, her eyes are looking up through that frozen dark sheet like she can still see the stars. And she stays there until the lake melts—which doesn't happen for like seventy-five years. But when it does, Astrid Dane just walks out like she's been taking a long bath.

"What was she thinking about for all that time?" Aubrey asks.

"I wondered the same thing," I say, and it comes out a little shaky and breathless because Aubrey *gets* Astrid Dane like I do.

Once we're on my street, I can see Gee's old dirty Mercedes in the driveway. And although I'm glad Gee's back, I'm not sure anymore about Aubrey coming over. I'm not sure how Aubrey and Gee would mix. I glance at Aubrey, wondering if there's a way to tell him he can't come over after all.

"My grandfather's home," I say.

"Oh, sway," Aubrey says.

"Maybe you should come over some other time?" I hate when I want to say something straight out, and it ends up sounding like a question. Like a choice.

"And miss meeting your grandpa? No way."

Aubrey walks ahead of me, like he's walking to his house instead of mine. And even though I can't see it, I just know his big old smile is spread across his face like honey on bread.

19

NERVOUS AND SIZZLING

As soon as I open the front door, jazz spills out of the house. Gee is serious about his music. Mama says that's where Malcolm gets it from, but jazz and hip-hop don't seem like the same thing at all to me.

I slide past Aubrey and hustle toward the kitchen. I know Gee's in there, probably humming to his music and starting something delicious for dinner.

I want to make sure I give Gee a heads-up about Aubrey before Gee says anything rude, but I'm not fast enough; Gee comes out of the kitchen carrying a plate of cheese and crackers.

"Nae-nae! Give me some sugar, girl." He sets the plate on the dining room table and holds his arms out so he can bury me in a big Gee hug, and I plant a loud smacking kiss on his cheek. Gee always says it's not a kiss at all if you can't hear it.

There's no sign of Malcolm; he's probably up in his room, drowning out Gee's music with his own.

"Gee, guess what? They're changing the name of our school." Even though I'm sure he's going to be mad my school won't be named after the Duke anymore, I'm still excited to tell him.

But before Gee can say anything, Aubrey interrupts. "They're *talking* about it."

Gee releases me and eyes Aubrey. "What have you gone and done to your hair?" he asks, as if he's known Aubrey forever.

I can feel my cheeks burning even though it's exactly what I've been wondering about.

Aubrey is smiling just as wide as ever, but he starts doing his hair-twisting thing, giving himself a tiny horn. I think it's what he does when he's nervous. Then he walks over to Gee and sticks out his hand. "Aubrey Banks, sir. A pleasure to meet you."

Gee looks at the hand for a moment longer than even I know is right, and then he shakes it, giving it a pretty hard squeeze, I guess, because Aubrey's smile gets shaky for a quick second.

"Gee, Aubrey is . . ." I lose my way right there. I don't have a single clue what Aubrey is. I look over at Aubrey for help, but his eyes are shining bright at me like he thinks this is pretty funny.

"Well, what is he?" Gee takes a step back, as if he needs to get a better look at Aubrey. "An alien? A cartoon character? A mythical creature from beyond?"

Aubrey laughs at my grandpa's ridiculousness. "No, sir. Just a . . ." He glances over at me, his eyes still twinkling. "Classmate of Nae-nae's."

I don't mind Gee's nickname for me, but I sure don't want *Aubrey* to call me that. It's private.

"*Jenae.*" I say my name loud enough to be heard right over the horns blowing from the stereo speakers. I don't know why I didn't think of the word *classmate*. And I don't know why I'm sort of mad that that's the word Aubrey picked.

"Well, classmate of *Jenae's*," Gee starts. "What's this about the school?"

I don't know why he's asking Aubrey when I was the one who told him the big news, even though technically, Aubrey said it better. So before Aubrey can answer, I say, "People don't like that it's named after John Wayne. They want to change it to a girl's name." I lose my way a bit because I can't remember the new name. "Sheila somebody?"

"Sylvia," Aubrey says. "Sylvia Mendez."

"What type of foolishness is that?" Gee asks.

"She was a big deal when she was a kid. Her parents sued the state . . . or something." Aubrey scratches his head, and I'm glad to see that he doesn't know everything. "But anyway, she got to go to a school that was supposed to be just for white kids. They had to integrate."

"Now I know that's plain wrong. *Brown versus Board of Education* did all that. What are they teaching you kids in that school?"

I've heard of that *Brown* case. Gee told me about it. He says it's important we know all about African American history. "Everybody knows *Brown* ended segregation," I tell Aubrey, and roll my eyes. "Click," I add, to show him how obvious the fact is.

"But Sylvia Mendez was before that," Aubrey says. He must see the disbelief in our faces, because he adds, "*Honest*. You can look it up online."

Gee narrows his eyes at that, like he thinks maybe Aubrey is being a little too smart.

Then Gee looks Aubrey up and down and asks, "All right, young blood, what exactly is going on with that hair?"

I hope Aubrey didn't think my grandpa was just going to give him a pass on the hair question. Gee is a dog with a bone when it comes to something he wants to know, and he never forgets.

"I dyed it," Aubrey says, and shrugs as if that explains everything.

I look back and forth between Aubrey and Gee, wondering if Gee is going to let it go or if he's going to press. Sometimes when Mama's family is all over, they'll start playing cards, and if they're playing whist, Gee will get a certain look before making his bid. He has the same look going now. But then he starts nodding to the music and snaps his fingers.

"Well, all right," he says, but I'm not sure if he's talking to Aubrey or the music.

"Is this Coltrane?" Aubrey asks.

Gee's eyes light up like a carnival ride. "You know your jazz, young man."

"My mom won't listen to anything else."

"Smart woman."

I'm not going to lie. I'm a little jealous. Gee is always trying to teach me about jazz, but I can't tell one artist from another. I know I like some of it. The smooth songs, like what's playing now. The ones that make you feel like it's a long summer day, with just the perfect cool breeze gliding over your skin. But some jazz is popcorn, jumping up and down, all nervous and sizzling.

Aubrey is nodding his head to the beat, and I am ready for him to leave. Sharing Astrid Dane is one thing, but sharing Gee is different.

"Is Malcolm upstairs?" I ask, glad that Gee turns back to me.

"Nope. Went to that PT. Grumbling the whole time he was fixing to go," Gee answers.

"That's great," I say. PT is physical therapy. And it's not great that Malcolm was grumbling, but it's good he went. He's supposed to go regularly, but he doesn't. Says it's stupid and hurts and is a waste of time. Something must've changed for him to have gone. I get a little tingle in my belly. Could my texts to Rox be working? Malcolm hasn't admitted to them being back in touch, but maybe she texted him after I told her about him feeling bad about their breakup. I hope he's not too stubborn to text her back. I want to text her again right now, but I don't want to do it in front of Aubrey.

"Y'all have homework or something you need to get to?" Gee asks. "Or you want a snack or something?" He gestures to the plate of cheese and crackers.

"Homework," I say, and head to the stairs.

"Oh, no, I don't think you young folks need to be upstairs.

You can do your homework right here where I can keep an eye on you. Don't need you up there messing around with each other. I'll turn the music down."

I can see that Gee has decided that this should be the most embarrassing day of my life.

20
EARLY HISTORY

Aubrey and I settle at the dining room table and find out even though we have math different periods, we both have Mr. Colson. So we decide to do math together. We zip through the math problems. I don't want to admit it, but it's nice having someone ask me how to solve for x. I love how logical math is, and how you get to solve tiny mini mysteries. What is x? How can you figure out y? All while we've been working, I heard his phone buzzing in his bag.

When it buzzes again, I give up trying to pretend I'm not curious and ask, "Don't you need to check your phone?"

"Naw, it's just my mom," Aubrey says. "She likes me to check in when she's at work." He pauses. "Or when she's not at work. Basically, all the time. I already answered her. But she keeps texting." He sounds exasperated.

As if she heard him talking about her, his phone buzzes again. I can't imagine ignoring Mama like that. "You better answer her," I say.

Aubrey says, "I did already."

But he takes his phone out and sends a quick text. "Satisfied?" he asks me.

I shrug. It doesn't matter to me one way or the other. I close my math book and take a mighty stretch.

Aubrey copies me, and then we both wiggle our arms around all goofy, making us both laugh.

"Can we take a break?" he asks.

The answer I want to say twists around in my mouth. Now that math is done, I think our studying should be over and Aubrey should just go ahead and go home.

At least that's what I think I want. But then Aubrey's smile gets smaller and he clears his throat and asks, "Or, um, you want me to leave?"

Instead of saying, *Yes, please*, my mouth decides on its own and says, "No, that's okay. Let's get another snack." We already plowed through the plate of cheese and crackers Gee laid out for us.

On our way to the kitchen I spy Gee through the French doors lining the back of the dining room. He's sitting under the fig tree in his "thinking chair." I hope he's not smoking. Mama has been after him forever to stop, and he tells her he's "just about" to quit, but sometimes I catch him having a smoke outside. Right now, though, it looks like he's just sitting there, pondering life.

"Um, do you like tortilla chips and salsa?" I ask Aubrey, already starting to pull the salsa out of the refrigerator.

"Yep. Maybe this is the moment I should tell you I like

pretty much everything! Name something you think I wouldn't want to eat."

"Anchovies."

"Yep."

"Brussels sprouts."

"Sautéed in garlic? Yum."

"Beets."

"Fresh, pickled, and baked. Yes, yes, yes."

I rack my brain for the worst possible thing. "Liver!"

But Aubrey nodded. "Oh, yeah, I am so into offal."

"Offal?"

"Organ meats. Kidneys and livers and tongue and—"

I wave my hands. "Stop! Stop! That's disgusting. It should be awful, not offal." I do a pretend gag.

Aubrey laughs at that. "I told you I like everything."

"You are *seriously* weird."

"Yeah, I know. But remember? My mom likes to cook, and the whole reason she's working in a restaurant is so she can work up to being a chef. That's why we moved here. She wanted to explore California cuisine."

"That's sway your mom wants to be a chef," I say.

Aubrey gets a goofy grin, and then he nods at me, and I nod back, and for a minute we're both just nodding and I have no idea what we're agreeing to.

By the time Gee comes back inside, Aubrey and I have settled at the kitchen island with chips and salsa and we have moved on to the super-boring history homework Mrs. Crawford assigned.

Aubrey is really good at finding where answers hide in text-books. We have almost all the questions answered, and if I had to do it by myself I would maybe have gotten to question four (*List at least two problems with the idea of manifest destiny*). Aubrey didn't even have to check the book for that one.

Gee picks up my history book and starts flipping through it. I know what he's looking for. A list of American presidents.

"It's *early* American history, Gee," I say. "We don't get to modern stuff until eighth grade."

He sucks his teeth at that. Mama said Gee cried when Barack Obama got elected president. He didn't think he'd live long enough to see a Black person elected president of the United States. Now he likes to check lists of presidents just to see Obama's name. He sets the book down and heads out to the living room.

Aubrey's phone buzzes again, and this time after he checks it, he says, "My mom just got off work. I better get home before she does." He gathers up his books, gives me a little two-finger salute, and then he's gone.

I really need to talk to him about how to say goodbye to people. Although I totally understand wanting to avoid getting in trouble for not being where you're supposed to be.

Gee's in the living room with the television blaring away. Instead of a Western, though, it's an infomercial selling some big toaster/barbecue/dehydration thing. I can't imagine Gee has any plans to buy something like that. "Are you watching this, Gee?"

"Huh?" he asks. "What now?"

He looks confused, so I point at the television. "This show. Is your movie over?"

Gee rubs his temples for a moment and then turns off the TV. "You know I'm not watching that silliness," he says, as if I had suggested he watch it. "Let me get to making something for dinner." He starts to get up, then sits back down with an *oof*.

"What's the matter?" I ask him.

"Just these old legs acting up," Gee says. "While I'm cooking, you look up that Mendez person on the computer. Man, that thing is smart."

Gee acts like computers have information tucked right inside them instead of being connected to the internet. He says he's too old to understand *all that malarkey*, but I know he's not too old. My great-uncle Bruce uses the internet all the time to keep up with basketball stats.

"Why don't we look it up together?" I'm trying to drag Gee into the twenty-first century whether he likes it or not. He doesn't like it.

He waves his arms at me and pulls himself out of the chair. "I don't got time for that. You just talk to that computer and see what it has to say." He points to the desktop computer tucked into a corner of the living room. Mama, Malcolm, and I all used it before my dad got me my laptop. Gee never uses it.

I roll my eyes at him, but I nod too. Gee lets us joke around with him, but at the end of the day, if he says jump, you better say, *How high?*

"I'll tell you what I find out," I say as he heads into the kitchen.

I start a search and quickly find out that Aubrey is right. There really was a case before *Brown v. Board of Education*. How can such a big deal have happened and I've never even heard of it? Especially when it happened in California?

When Sylvia Mendez was in third grade, her parents wanted her to go to the school near their house. Problem was, that school was just for white kids and Sylvia's family was Mexican and Puerto Rican. Sylvia's cousins got to go to the school because they were light skinned enough to look white, but Sylvia and her brothers were darker. The school district said they had to go to a school for Mexican kids. But Sylvia's parents, they wanted their kids to go to the school that was close by in their own neighborhood, and they were willing to make a big deal about it.

Most of the pictures of Sylvia are when she's a grown-up, but there's one of her as a kid. She looks nice, but very, very serious. I wonder if she wanted to go to that school for white kids. Can you imagine being only eight and going to school knowing a whole bunch of people didn't want you there? I'm eleven and I don't think I could do it. And Sylvia couldn't make herself invisible—she just had to go to her classes, holding her books and lunch tight, and hope no one did more than name-calling. She must've been really brave.

It would be awful knowing people didn't want you around.

That's how her case was won. The judge said schools shouldn't make kids feel bad about who they are. And even though the school district appealed and tried to have the ruling overturned, a whole bunch of lawyers said they thought the first ruling should stand. Before he won the *Brown v. Board of Education* case and before he was a Supreme Court justice, Thurgood Marshall was one of those lawyers who helped make sure the court didn't change its mind. He said how important it was for Sylvia to be allowed to go to the school her parents wanted her to. He must've done a good job writing up his opinion, because another court said the first decision was right: Sylvia, and kids like her, could go to the school near them even if it used to be only for white kids.

I like the idea of people coming together for a good cause. Maybe I should go into the kitchen to help Gee and tell him what I found out, especially since Gee was the one who told me about Thurgood Marshall and how he was the first Black judge to be on the US Supreme Court. But Mama isn't home yet, and I can probably get away with watching at least one Astrid Dane video.

A new video got posted less than half an hour ago! I want to click on it and watch it, but I also want to wait. This is what always happens. It could be weeks before another new episode gets posted. And sometimes waiting in between is so hard I can't stand it. So I try to put off watching for as long as I can to draw it out.

My finger rests on the enter button, and I gnaw on the inside of my cheek, wondering how long I can hold out, and then I double-click. I've never been able to wait more than a few seconds.

I wonder if Aubrey is watching right now too.

21

DON'T WORRY

In the morning, everything I put on seems wrong. Usually I don't care what I wear, but maybe Mama's right about me needing to dress more like everyone else. I put on the sparkly sweatshirt she got me, but the sequins are just too much. If you've ever been invisible, you know sequins have no place in that business.

When Mama shouts for me to hurry up, I pull on a blue T-shirt that used to be Malcolm's. It's too big, but it's soft and has a picture of Bob Marley on it, and whenever I wear it, I sing to myself, *Don't worry about a thing. 'Cause every little thing's gonna be all right.*

I don't know many Bob Marley songs, but I love that one. If you sing it enough, you really can make yourself believe everything is going to be fine.

Downstairs, I grab an apple and follow Mama out the door. I'm already in the car before I realize I didn't make myself a lunch.

Mama must realize the same thing, because she tells me to

go into her purse and pull out five dollars so I can buy today.

I don't want to go to the cafeteria at lunchtime. But I take the money and smoosh it into my pocket.

"Mama, do you ever wish you lived in another time?"

"What?"

"You know, like if you could pick. Go back a hundred years, or two hundred. Would you?"

"So I could be a slave? No, thank you!"

Astrid Dane was born hundreds of years ago, all the way back in the 1600s, so of course she was around during slavery times. In one of the episodes, she was actually a slave. But she ran away. It helped that she could do stuff like stay underwater until dogs got tired and her master figured she'd drowned. She didn't stay in America after that.

Those are the types of things Mama loses patience with about Astrid Dane. She's all like "Really? A kid can just leave America and escape to a whole other *continent*?"

I don't point out that it's a lot easier to do that on an animated show, because then Mama would just rattle off her low opinion of "cartoons."

Sometimes I wonder if Astrid Dane gets tired. Living for hundreds and hundreds of years like that? I love everything about Astrid Dane, but I wouldn't want to be immortal. One lifetime is enough.

"Okay, Mama, say you could live in any century and in any part of the world, so you wouldn't have to be a slave. What then?"

"Jenae, you're going to give me a headache."

"Come on, Mama."

Mama taps her fingernails on the steering wheel. I don't think she's going to answer, because she doesn't like to play along when I start wondering what she calls outlandish things, but then she says, "Egypt, back when there were pharaohs? I wouldn't mind seeing just how they built those pyramids. And seeing brown folks in charge? Shoot, sign me right up for that."

"Me too," I say, shocked that Mama picks the exact time and place I would pick.

"Then I guess you'd still be my daughter," Mama says with a smile.

Mama isn't sweet all that often, but it sure sounds like she's saying I'm her daughter no matter what, and that makes me feel like one of those gooey candies with the sugary burst of flavor inside just exploded in my mouth.

I'm feeling so good, I make the mistake of asking a question Mama doesn't like. "Do you think Malcolm is going to be okay?" I don't look at her when I ask, because I'm hoping she'll lie to me, and I don't want to see the truth written all over her face.

"That boy will be fine once he realizes basketball isn't the end all be all. Best way to lose yourself is thinking you only got one dream in this world." Her voice isn't sweet anymore, and the deliciousness I was feeling evaporates.

I look at her. She has an angry/sad face going strong. It's not one or the other. "So you don't think he'll be able to play anymore? His knee isn't going to get better? The surgery didn't fix it?" At each question, more and more of my breath slips away until I'm almost gasping.

"I don't know, Jenae. The doctors don't know either. All I know is he best not give up on living if he can't ball."

"Having a dream is important, though," I say.

"Did you hear me say it wasn't? But *one* dream? Like there's only one thing in the world that can make you happy? That doesn't make any kind of sense. That's believing in that soulmate, happily-ever-after garbage." She cuts her eyes at me, but then she surprises me by smiling. "I know you're too smart for that."

I'm definitely not too smart for anything.

I give Mama a kiss goodbye and scoot out the car. The people with fliers are back, but now the people with signs supporting the name change are there too.

The two groups are making a point of not standing near each other.

Mama keeps her window rolled up and doesn't take a flier.

A man with a huge beard hands me one and says, "Support the Duke!"

I'm not sure if I'm supposed to say anything back, and I look uneasily at the people with signs. I don't want them to think I'm taking sides. My mouth gets dry like someone stuffed cotton balls in there.

"Jenae! Jenae!" a voice hollers, and the cotton dissolves.

"Hey, Aubrey," I say, turning away from the man. I can't

help smiling, because if I thought Aubrey's smile was big before, it's nothing like it is now.

"Did you see it?" he just about shouts at me.

I nod happily, too full of the thrill of sharing the excitement of a new Astrid Dane episode with someone to put words together.

Aubrey is practically jumping up and down like he's a piece of popcorn in some hot oil.

"I watched it three times!" he says.

"Four," I admit. When you don't know when you're going to get a new video, you have to watch a new one over and over. I mean you really *have* to.

"I knew you'd beat me," Aubrey says, like he doesn't mind. Like me watching more times than him is better than the other way around.

Almost everything about Aubrey surprises me. He's not quite like anyone else. He's a jigsaw puzzle piece that doesn't fit into any of the empty spaces.

"Come on, let's get to class!" he says, and even though he's talking loud and being the opposite of invisible, I stick next to him all the way to history.

22

NO BIG DEAL

All those people in the front of the school are hard to ignore, and Mrs. Crawford spends the first ten minutes of class talking to us about Sylvia Mendez. "The reason not as many people are familiar with her," Mrs. Crawford explains, "is because Sylvia Mendez's case was argued in the *California* Supreme Court, not the United States Supreme Court. It took *Brown versus Board of Education* to end segregated schools across the country."

I'm glad Gee had me do that research, because it makes me feel smart to already know this stuff about Sylvia Mendez.

Mrs. Crawford tells us how the Mendez case was a really important moment in California's history. And how Sylvia Mendez received the Presidential Medal of Freedom when Obama was president for the work she did to ensure all children have equal education opportunities.

I guess there's no way to go through what Sylvia did as a kid and not keep thinking about it for the rest of your life.

Addyson Gentry blurts out, "She sounds cool and all, but

our school has always been John Wayne. Why can't they just name a *new* school after her?"

Aubrey flings his arm up, but Mrs. Crawford ignores him.

"Partly because new schools don't get built all that often," she tells Addyson.

Aubrey starts waving his arm around like he's on fire. Of course, everyone turns around to stare. I press back in my seat and lower my head. Aubrey just doesn't know how to do things quietly.

"Yes?" Mrs. Crawford asks with a tightness in her voice, as if she's exhausted by Aubrey.

"Just because something has always been one way doesn't mean it should stay that way," Aubrey says. "And if one of your friends started saying all sorts of bad stuff about you, would you still want to be friends with them? *I* wouldn't. And I don't think we should want to go to a school named after someone like that."

"What do you mean?" a boy calls out. "What did John Wayne say?"

Mrs. Crawford's cheeks get pink, and she grips the back of her chair like she needs some support.

Aubrey is just about bouncing in his seat. "A bunch of racist—"

Mrs. Crawford cuts Aubrey off. "*Thank* you, Aubrey." She sounds like she's putting a period on the conversation, so I think she's going to change the subject, but instead she says, "John

Wayne publicly questioned the intelligence of Black people, and he suggested that Native people were selfish to want to hold on to their land. He stated his belief in white supremacy." Mrs. Crawford's cheeks have gone from pink to red. "And while it can be argued that it was a different time, it could also be argued that that's exactly why things should change. Most of us would like to believe people don't think like that anymore. And to have a school in this neighborhood be more reflective of the community would be a good thing." She smiles, and I notice some kids are sitting up straighter and nodding, like they think it would be a good thing too.

Mrs. Crawford claps her hands, signaling the discussion is over. "Let's get back to the gold rush! Take out your homework, everyone."

Aubrey nudges my foot with his, like I might've forgotten we did our homework together.

For the first time, I get all the answers on my history homework right.

When we leave class, Aubrey says, "See you later!" Then he starts down the hall, and it's not until he has almost disappeared into the sea of students that I realize I didn't tell him I would be eating in the cafeteria.

My mouth goes dry. I can still see his bright red hair, and if I shouted his name, he'd probably hear me, but I don't. Other people can be loud and shout to their friends, but I can't do that. His name is tied up and tangled in my mouth and refuses to come out, and before I can do anything about it, he's gone.

I tell myself it's no big deal. He probably won't even care. And he'll just go hang out with all the friends I'm sure he's made in his other classes. I bet he has tons of people asking him to sit with them at lunch. He's not like me with no friends. But even though I don't even want to sit with anyone at lunch, it would probably hurt my feelings if I thought someone was going to meet up with me and just didn't show.

So, in second period, I decide that at the beginning of lunch I'll just run over to the spot behind the container and wait for Aubrey, and then we can go together to the cafeteria.

But in third period, that doesn't seem like such a great idea. What if he doesn't even really want to sit with me at lunch? Maybe he just felt sorry for me when he saw me sitting by myself. Maybe he wasn't even talking about lunch when he said *later* and was really talking about fifth period.

By fourth period I've convinced myself Aubrey won't care. Why would he? We're not *really* friends. We both just like Astrid Dane. But he calls himself a Danish, and I don't. And he's loud like he wants to be heard. He *likes* giving speeches and debating and all that. Besides, he has that wild hair. You definitely want to be seen with hair that color. If we were truly friends, he would at least tell me why he dyes his hair neon red; he knows I want to know, but he won't tell me. Then there's him being all into jazz and offal, which is just too strange for a seventh grader. No, we definitely aren't friends, and not meeting up with him is no big deal.

23

EVERYONE ELSE

I hate the cafeteria.

There are long lines for food, no matter what you want to buy. Even if you just want a burrito or slice of pizza. The line for the full lunch is the shortest, but I can't stand the thought of eating those runny mashed potatoes, canned veggies, and chicken nuggets that look hard and dry.

I keep checking the big clock on the wall as if I'm late for something. Every time I see five more minutes pass, I picture Aubrey over by the container, wondering where I am, and thinking I'm kind of a jerk for not being there.

When I finally get my soggy, leaking burrito, I stare at all the tables, wondering where to sit. We've only been in school for a week and it seems like everyone is already set. No one else is standing with their food, not knowing where to go. Everyone else is scarfing down their lunch, or still in line, or laughing, or throwing peas, or holding hands. Everyone else belongs somewhere.

I would just take my food outside, but I saw the sign when I walked in:

ALL CAFETERIA FOOD MUST BE EATEN
IN THE CAFETERIA

Who came up with that dumb rule?

A girl with a bright pink sweatshirt emblazoned with magenta sequins spelling out L-O-V-E bumps into me. It's the same sweatshirt Mama bought me.

"Sorry," she says. "Didn't see you." She dashes to a loud table full of laughing girls, all wearing bright colors. The table is like a garden sprouting in the middle of the beige-and-gray cafeteria.

I head away from that table, to the first empty chair I see, squeeze a packet of hot sauce on my burrito, and slump over my plate. I don't look at anyone. No one says anything to me. I have settled into invisibility. And it's not hard, but it doesn't feel as good as it normally does.

I chew as quietly as I can and stare at the clock. Ten more minutes of lunch. That means that if Aubrey went behind the container, he's been wondering where I am for thirty minutes. And I know even if we aren't friends, and even if maybe he didn't really mean he was going to meet me at lunch when he said *later*, I should've gone over there first before the cafeteria.

I know something else too. I'm scared to see his face in English. Scared that instead of his usual smile, he's going to have a big, fat frown and it's going to be aimed right at me.

24
THE OPPOSITE OF FUN

When I get to English, Aubrey's already in his seat. I glance over, and he's not frowning. But he's not smiling either. I look away fast.

Mr. Humphries announces he's going to change up our persuasive speech assignment a little. "I am going to make this assignment a lot of fun! Instead of individual speeches, I'm going to have you partner up, and you and your partner will take different sides of the argument. One of you will argue for something, and the partner will argue against it."

For an English teacher, Mr. Humphries is not very good at words, because he clearly doesn't know the meaning of the word *fun*. But when I look back at Aubrey, he has a *huge* grin on his face like Mr. Humphries's news is the best thing.

"*And*," Mr. Humphries says, then pauses dramatically like he's ready to deliver the most wonderfullest thing ever. My stomach sinks to my knees, because I know whatever he's about to say is not going to be wonderful at all. "Some of you may not know this, but I run the debate club. It's quite popular, and it's really just for eighth graders, but as a special incentive for you all to do well on this project, I'm going to let two people who do the very best job join the club if they'd like. Members of the debate club are eligible to go to debate camp in the summer. You're going to want to get picked just for that alone! I'm going to ask some of the club members to come watch the speeches to help me judge. So work hard, all right?" He grins broadly at us, and I frown back.

None of his news makes the assignment fun. It is the opposite of fun.

"We're doing debates?" Aubrey calls out, sounding excited.

I kick one of the legs of my desk. Of course Aubrey would be happy about this. He's probably already imagining all his new friends on the debate club.

Mr. Humphries shakes his head slowly. "I'm hesitant to call these debates, because there are very specific rules governing those. But in the very loosest definition of the word, yes, you and your partner will debate a topic. Make sense?" He pauses, and even though no one says anything, he says, "Great. You can talk after class about who you're going to partner up with."

I stare hard at my desk. I can't see it, but I know all around me people are doing that partnering-up thing, catching the eyes of the person they want to work with. I know no one wants to be my partner. Not after the horrendous job I did the first day in class. As much as I don't want to give any type of speech *ever*,

I can't help but feel sad knowing no one wants to be my partner. Maybe if I had met up with Aubrey at lunch, he'd be grinning at me, letting me know we're a set.

After class, I hear someone calling Aubrey's name, and I know they want to be partners with him. I don't stick around to see how no one is calling my name. I doubt any of my class-mates *know* my name, or even see me. Or if they do, they see the worst speech giver in the history of the world.

When I leave sixth period, I don't wait around to see if Aubrey appears; I just start my walk home, moving as fast as I can. I check behind me a few times to see if Aubrey is following me, or even just going the same way I am. I don't see him. And trust me, I'd see that red hair if he was anywhere around.

He seemed so excited about Mr. Humphries's idea about the debate speeches. How can he and I be so different? And more important, how can I get out of giving my side of a stupid speech?

Almost as soon as I ask myself the question, the beginning of an idea starts to squirm around in my brain. An awful idea. A really bad, horrible idea that just might work.

25

A BAD IDEA

The busy part of the neighborhood falls behind me as I turn off to the quiet streets, and I start wondering about the people who live in the houses and what makes some people not care about weeds getting so tall they're as high as my waist, while other people keep their yards so tidy, it looks like they might get outside with a vacuum cleaner and mop and duster. I wonder about all that mainly so I don't have to think about getting out of the speech. But the idea is like a weed. Growing fast and pokey with barbs.

Mama will be really mad if she finds out, but since she tries to avoid talking to my dad as much as possible, she probably never would. Still, the idea makes my neck sweat and my breath come out hard and too fast.

Normally, it bothers me that my dad barely ever comes around. He says it's because he travels so much, but it feels like he just doesn't want to see me. For my plan to work, though, it's a good thing that I can count on him not coming over.

But if Mama finds out my dad did me a favor without her

knowing about it—especially *this* favor—they will get into one huge monster of an argument. And it will be all my fault.

So I better make double, triple sure I don't get caught.

Since it's Friday, Mama comes home early and I act extra sweet to her, because I'm feeling guilty. I ask her lots of times what I can do to help get things ready for the fish fry.

Most Friday nights, Mama's family comes over for fried fish. Nana June started it, so it's always been right here. She liked having all her kids (and their kids) over. But even though she lives in Florida now, we keep having the fish fries here. Makes sense. It's the biggest house in the family, with enough room for everyone to fit. We have Thanksgiving and Christmas here too.

For someone who doesn't cook that often, Mama sure can cook up some catfish and shrimp. Sometimes she makes a pot of greens too, but usually she'll just do the fish, and Uncle AJ brings huge bags of french fries, and Auntie Maug makes a salad (or makes me do it), and there's always garlic bread dripping with butter.

I think it makes Gee happy to look around the table and see all the people who wouldn't even exist if it weren't for him and Nana June getting married a million years ago. Used to be my cousins would come over too, but they're all older than Malcolm and me, so most Fridays they usually are off doing things with their friends. I don't get how anyone would choose to miss out on a fish fry.

"You want me to set the table, Mama? Or make some iced tea?"

"Jenae, stop bothering me. You're like a hummingbird tonight, zipping around my head!"

"I'm just trying to help." I pout.

"June, stop fussing at the girl!" Gee hollers, and rubs a knuckle between his eyebrows. "Making this headache worse with that noise."

"*You* have a headache?" Mama demands. "Try working all day and then having to do everything. And for the record, my name is *Mona*."

Gee just stares at her for a second, then shakes his head. "I know your name, girl! This darn headache is just muddling things. And watch your tone."

Mama looks like she's about to argue, but then she just says, "I'm going upstairs to get comfortable before I start frying up the catfish. Jenae, get out the plates and napkins, and, Daddy, take some aspirin."

"Okay, Mama!" I say, happy to have a job. For the holidays, we get out the fancy dishes, but for fish fries, it's a stack of paper plates and a ton of napkins. "You want me to get you something for your headache, Gee?" I ask, before heading into the kitchen.

"Naw, I'm just going to settle in my chair. Watch my program before the house fills up." Gee sits down and turns on the television, putting on a Western, of course, but then he closes his eyes instead of watching.

I go into the kitchen to start getting things ready for Mama. As I set out the plates and napkins and get out stuff Mama will need, like the oil and flour, I catch myself thinking about Aubrey.

As much as I love our Friday dinners, I wish it wasn't Friday yet. I won't see Aubrey until Monday. That's two days stretched between us with me not being able to say anything about lunch today and how I'll be back by the container Monday. What if during those two empty days, he realizes he's better off hanging with someone else at lunch? Like whoever he partnered up with in English?

My elbow hits the bag of flour, and it falls on the floor with a big thump. Flour explodes into the air.

It is literally snowing in the kitchen. Mama is going to kill me.

The unsettled flour makes my eyes sting and water, but I can't just stand there crying over spilled flour.

I get a big pot from the cabinet and slide the busted bag of flour into it. Okay.

And then I start sweeping. It doesn't seem to matter how much I sweep, though—the flour is still everywhere. Even wet paper towels don't do that great a job.

If Aubrey were here, I bet he'd have an idea of how to clean all this up.

That is a silly thing to think, and I get annoyed with myself. Why would Aubrey be here?

I get the vacuum cleaner out of the small hall closet right when Mama comes back down the stairs.

"What in God's green acres did you do to yourself?" she asks.

Gee's eyes pop open at her question and he takes one look at me, says, "Lord," and closes his eyes again.

Mama pushes past me to the kitchen, and when she sees the disaster I made, she whips around so fast, I'm surprised she doesn't fall.

"Jenae!" She grabs the vacuum out of my hands and goes back into the kitchen. It all happens so fast, I don't have a second to explain. And then I look at my arms. See the fine white pre-sifted flour, sticking to each hair.

Great. And, of course, that's right when the front door opens and my aunts and uncles start piling in.

The thing about living in Gee's house is, all of Mama's siblings have a key, since they used to live here. And it's not like we can complain. It's as much their house as it is ours. But talk about something making Mama mad. When Auntie Jackie brought over a bunch of dresses and just shoved them into the closet in a spare room Mama was using for extra storage, and smooshed waves of wrinkles into Mama's clothes, Mama just about lost it.

I dissolve into the wall and let the shadows melt over me. At least it's easy to be invisible with Mama's family. Their loudness covers me like a blanket. Everyone is too busy talking over everyone else to worry about me.

Then the doorbell rings, and no one goes to answer it, and it rings again, so I push myself out of the shadows and go open the door.

"Aubrey?" Even though that bright red hair is blinding me, I can't quite believe he's standing there. "What . . . are you doing here?"

"Better question," he says. "What happened to you?"

26
WHAT HAPPENED WAS

"I didn't have time to make my lunch. I had to buy. I was in the cafeteria." The words bubble out of me like a shaken-up soda.

He stares at me for a second before saying, "I mean, what happened to you? You're covered in . . ." He leans close and peers at my arm. "Flour?"

I step outside and close the door behind me. I go over to the water hose and rinse the flour off my arms and splash water on my face, then rub it off with my shirt. "Better?" I ask.

Aubrey shrugs. "I don't know, I kinda liked the ghost look." His smile eats up his entire face, and that makes me smile too.

"I dropped a bag of flour, and it exploded," I say. I wish that's what I had said when I first opened my mouth. "It got all over the kitchen."

"And you."

"And me."

We stand there, quiet, a road going one way, and a road going another, and neither of us seeming to know where to put our feet, or even if we remember how to walk.

"So, the cafeteria?" he asks.

I give him three fast nods. "I should've— I didn't want you to—" I dust flour from my T-shirt. "What *are* you doing here?"

Aubrey looks up at the clouds for a minute. "When you didn't show up for lunch, I wondered if maybe I was a little too . . . um, in your space?" He glances at me quick and then back up at the clouds. He shoves his hands in his jeans pockets and rocks back on his heels.

"My mom tells me I can be sort of intense?" He gives me another quick glance.

Maybe I'm supposed to disagree with him.

"The thing is . . . back in Chicago, I . . . I didn't . . . It's not . . ." He pauses and pulls a hand out of his pocket and starts doing the hair-twist thing he does.

I don't know what he's trying to say, and he looks so uncertain, I'm not sure if he knows either. "It's not, what?" I ask.

He grins self-consciously. "It's just that . . . I guess I can overdo it sometimes. I just wanted to come over and let you know it was okay if you wanted me to leave you alone at lunch." He says that last bit in a big rush, and his hair twisting goes into overdrive. He doesn't look at me but stares at his yellow Vans instead.

"No, that's okay," I say, talking as fast as Aubrey. "I mean, it's a free country. You can sit wherever you want." I think I made him feel bad, and that makes *me* feel bad, but I don't want to go all overboard and seem like a big weirdo or anything.

Aubrey stops twisting, looks up at me, and takes a step back.

He seems to be waiting for something. "Oh, okay, then." He starts to turn away.

"Wait!" I shout at him, making him jump. "You don't have to leave." I pinch hard right between my thumb and index finger, forcing myself to stay there. Not letting myself disappear. "And you're not *that* intense."

Something crashes inside, and I groan. I bet one of my goofball uncles broke something. "You want to come in?"

I've never seen a smile that big.

"Let me just text my mom so she doesn't freak out," he says.

27

JUST OLD

Inside, I tell Aubrey I'll be back in a second and then I run upstairs to get out of my messed-up clothes. Flour drifts behind me like fog.

When I get to my room, I finally have a chance to look in a mirror. Flour is all in my hair. I look like I got cast in the role of Grandma in a play. The thought makes me giggle and reminds me of an Astrid Dane episode where she tried her best to look older. She wore makeup and heels and looked ridiculous.

I do the best job I can to get all the flour off me, moving as fast as I can, not wanting Aubrey to have to deal with my family by himself.

A lot of laughter and yelling is going on—which is how it usually sounds on a Friday night—but my aunties and uncles might be too much for Aubrey. If he thought *he* could be a little intense.

I race back downstairs, expecting everyone to be surrounding Aubrey in a tight circle, tossing questions at him one after another like hot darts, but they're not. They're all too busy settling into their standard fussing routines. Mama says it just goes with the territory that with so many of them, she and her siblings are going to be at each other all the time, but sometimes it seems like they don't agree on anything.

I don't even see Aubrey. Maybe he left. The idea makes me feel hollow.

Malcolm is sitting next to Uncle AJ, deep in conversation, and I hear Uncle AJ tell Malcolm about sticking with physical therapy. Uncle AJ should know, because he played football in college and got banged up a bunch. He had to do a lot of PT, according to Mama. He's tried to talk to Malcolm before, but usually Malcolm avoids him. Now Malcolm's listening and nodding, and a tiny sliver of hope squeezes down my spine. I ask Malcolm if he knows where Aubrey is, and he points toward the French doors in the dining room that lead outside.

I go over and stare out, finding Aubrey easily. He would lose every time in hide-and-go-seek with that hair. He's sitting next to Gee, and whatever Aubrey is saying, it is making Gee crack up. I watch them for a minute, not jealous exactly, but wondering what it might feel like to be that easy with people. Then I open up the door and go outside.

"Hey, Gee," I call, and he beckons me.

"Come on over here, Nae-nae," he says. "Can you believe this boy has the good common sense to like chitlins?"

Gee and I argue about chitterlings. I'm not even going to

tell you what part of a pig's body they come from. That's how gross it is. I wrinkle up my nose. "That's 'cause he likes *everything*. It doesn't count."

Aubrey smiles at me, like he's glad I know this fact about him.

Gee chuckles, and Aubrey says, "No, but they're good. Seriously."

"Your *offal* opinion can't be trusted," I joke, and Gee and Aubrey both bust up laughing.

Aubrey leans back in the chair and says, "It sure is nice out here. We lived in the city in an apartment. No trees to climb." He looks at the huge avocado tree longingly, probably imagining himself climbing way up.

Our backyard is full of all sorts of fruit trees. Cherry, fig, peach, apricot, orange, and avocado.

"Gee planted all of these. Even the avocado. He said it was tiny when he planted it, right, Gee?"

Gee doesn't answer, and when I look over at him, it doesn't seem like he's even listening.

"Hey, Gee, you want us to pick some apples for you? I bet you'd like some apple pie."

He doesn't answer again, so I holler, "Hey, Gee!" at him. His head turns my way, and for a second I think his face looks strange. His eyes seem too small, and his cheeks are sunken in. He looks like he's aged fifty years. But then he blinks a bunch of times and he goes back to being Gee.

"Come on, y'all, let's pick some of these apples," he says, but his voice doesn't sound right, like it's snagging on something. "Maybe someone will make me a pie." He gets up and rubs his leg and then gives it a few whacks. "Darn leg," he says. Then he shakes his head. "Let me get the ladder." He heads behind the garage, and it seems to me that he's walking a little wobbly.

"Is he okay?" Aubrey asks, and I don't know why, but it makes me mad.

"Yes," I say. "He's fine!" I start picking the apples I can reach.

"Okay," Aubrey says, and joins me, but most of them are growing too high, so we have to wait for Gee to come back with the ladder, but he doesn't.

"He's probably sneaking a smoke," I say, but after another few minutes, when Gee still doesn't come back, I shrug at Aubrey and go looking for him, with Aubrey trailing me. We find Gee behind the garage, rubbing his leg again.

"Gee!" I call out. "Aren't you going to bring us the ladder?"

He gives his leg a shake. "Leg didn't want to cooperate." He pauses and takes a few deep breaths. "Just . . . went . . . goofy on me." He is smiling, but he doesn't sound very jokey, and his voice sounds slow, as if he has to take too many breaths.

The ladder is resting on the ground behind him, so Aubrey and I run over and pick it up together. It's not very heavy, but it is long, and it's nice to have a helper to carry it. Gee leans against the garage wall.

"You okay, Gee?" I ask before Aubrey and I turn the corner of the garage.

Gee runs a hand over his face and gives his leg another shake. Then he grins at me. "Sure enough. Just old." And he sounds like himself again, so I stop worrying.

He follows me and Aubrey back to the apple tree.

Aubrey uses the ladder to climb right up. I climb after him, and we swing and climb through the tree like he's Spider-Man and I'm Astrid Dane.

28

LEAVE THE NAME ALONE

When we finally head back inside for dinner, we have a whole bucket filled with apples and are covered in dirt and scratches.

Mama picks a leaf out of my hair and frowns. "Go wash up," she says, and gives me one of those looks that means I need to use one of my freshening wipes to get the stink and sweat off me.

Upstairs, the smell of the food makes me wash up extra fast. Garlic and lemon and cayenne pepper. The fishy smell of catfish and the almost-metal smell of shrimp. Even the flour has a smell once it hits the sizzling-hot oil. It's like clean, moist earth.

"Check the bread!" someone shouts. There's been enough times when the bread got forgotten in the broiler and came out as smoky black bricks. I hustle downstairs, but Auntie Jackie is already pulling the perfectly toasted bread out of the oven.

When all the food is ready, we cram around the dining room table and Uncle Deon says a quick funny prayer about loaves and fishes, and then we all dig in. My favorite thing is to take a piece of garlic bread, pile about four or five shrimp on top of it, and fold it in half for a garlicky shrimp sandwich. Talk about good eating.

Aubrey piles his plate high with everything, and it's not until we both have our mouths full of food that it occurs to anyone that me having a guest over for Friday fish fry is something unusual.

"Y'all go to school together?"

"How come we've never met you before?"

"Your mama lets you dye your hair like that?"

"How long you been knowin' Jenae?"

"What's your name, son?"

"Where are your people from?"

The questions come like a sudden hailstorm, and I can't even keep up with who's asking what. I half expect Aubrey to start ducking. But he just answers them one by one. "Yes, we have two classes together. I just moved here. Yes, she lets me. I met Jenae on the first day of school. Aubrey. I'm from Chicago, and I guess my people are from there too." He glances over at me, and I think he's asking me if he did okay, so I give him a little nod.

"Nice to meet a friend of Jenae's," Auntie Maug says, sounding a little sad.

But after that, Mama's family is too interested in who said what to whom, and who went to the doctor recently, and whose ex-wife called and whose kids are messing up, to bother with Aubrey anymore.

After an overly detailed talk about Uncle Corvis's kidney

stones, Auntie Maug tells Malcolm, "Doctors don't know everything! Great-Uncle Jas swore by cod-liver oil and fifty squats a day. Lived to a hundred."

Malcolm's eyebrows press together. "You think some fish oil is going to fix my knee?"

Auntie Maug is always spewing out home remedies, but this sounds ridiculous. She must think so too, because she cracks up laughing. "Oh, now, give me some credit, Malcolm. I know you needed the surgery, but now you gotta think about recovery and getting stronger. Cod-liver oil." She nods decisively. "That's the answer."

Seeing the angry look on Malcolm's face makes sweat sprout on my nose. *Don't ruin it!* I want to shout at Auntie Maug. I should've tried to get Rox over tonight. She used to always come over for fish fries. Malcolm would be laughing instead of looking like he has something burning inside of him.

Uncle AJ holds a hand up at Malcolm, as if he can sense that Malcolm is about to get rude, and changes the subject. "Hey, Pops," he says. "You hear about Jenae's school? Them changing the name from John Wayne to Sylvia Mendez?"

"Plain foolishness," Gee says, and reaches for more garlic bread. He shakes his head before taking a big bite.

"If they're looking for a new name, why not Malcolm X or Barack Obama? Shoot, even *Michelle* Obama!" Uncle Phil says.

"Babe, you know nobody thinks anybody Black 'ceptin' Dr. King needs a school named after them," Auntie Jackie tells Uncle Phil. She's always talking politics and going to protests.

I think about telling them what I learned about Sylvia Mendez, but I stay quiet.

"Have you paid attention to who is living in this neighborhood now?" Uncle AJ says. "It ain't white anymore, but it sure ain't Black neither. Mexican. That's what it is."

"*Latinx*," Mama and Auntie Jackie say at the exact same time, and Uncle AJ throws his hands up like he's saying, *Don't shoot.*

"Not every brown person you see is Mexican, AJ," Auntie Jackie says. "Maybe you should talk to people. My Zumba instructor is from El Salvador. My boss is from Nicaragua. The dude down—"

"Okay, Jack!" Uncle AJ says. "I got it."

Uncle Phil laughs. "I still think it should be Michelle Obama Junior High."

"What they need to do is leave the name alone," Gee says gruffly. "The Duke was the greatest."

Uncle Phil says, "Muhammad Ali was the greatest."

"John Wayne wouldn't have let us sit at his table," Auntie Denise says.

Gee shakes his head at that. "Shoot, y'all don't know what you're talking about. John Wayne stood up for the little man."

"Yeah, in *movies*," Auntie Jackie argues. "Didn't you hear about that interview he did back in the day? Saying all that nonsense about how we weren't capable. And he was all up in that business with people getting blacklisted in Hollywood. Calling everybody a communist. It's all online, Daddy."

"Online this and online that," Gee says. "Time to be off-line if you ask me. What's past is past. Let the man rest in peace."

"Come on, Dad, wouldn't you want to see Jenae going to a school named after a person of color?" Auntie Maug asks.

Gee rubs his chin for a minute, glances at me, then looks back down at his food. I'm not used to seeing him like that. He's usually so sure about everything.

My mouth fills with words to say to my family, about how they should leave Gee alone, and how it's my school, so why should they care, but I don't make a peep. They wouldn't listen to me anyway.

29
WHAT SIDE DO YOU WANT?

After dinner, Aubrey and I go sit at the computer in the living room and watch the Astrid Dane video. You would think neither of us had seen it before.

Gee is in his big chair, reclined back, with a Western on, of course, but it's not a John Wayne one, and I wonder if Gee wishes it was. My uncles, Malcolm, and Auntie Jackie are still at the dining room table throwing bones. Gee told me dominoes are called bones because they used to be actually made of bone. The dominoes are thrown down so hard, I'm surprised they don't shatter.

Mama and my other aunties have disappeared into the kitchen to gossip. Auntie Jackie always says she's "not about that sexist nonsense" whenever "the girls" go to the kitchen.

I turn back to the computer. "What do you think is going to happen?" I ask Aubrey, once we've watched it twice. "How is she going to escape?"

Aubrey asks for a piece of paper and draws a quick sketch of Astrid Dane.

"You draw good," I tell him.

"My mom says people are usually good at stuff they like to do," Aubrey says, like it's no big deal. Then he rubs his belly. "Dinner was so good! And your family gave me an idea of a great topic for our debate. We can do the school name change."

For a sliver of a second, I'm so happy that Aubrey didn't partner up with anybody else I forget to be terrified about giving a speech, but then that part comes back. "You don't really want to be my partner. I'm no good at speeches." I don't add that if my idea works, I won't even be there to give the speech.

"That's okay. I'll help you, and you'll get better. We can both be in the debate club!"

I don't know what would give Aubrey the idea that I'd want

to be in the debate club. I shake my head hard. "I can't do it."

"Can."

Just the thought makes my tongue feel too big for my mouth. Sweat pings out all over me, and my throat squeezes closed. I shake my head hard. "You should pick somebody else," I say in a narrow voice.

Gee coughs loudly, making me and Aubrey both turn to look at him. "Gotta stop being afraid of things, Nae-nae," he says. "Once you do the thing you're afraid of? Shoot, no one can mess with you after that."

"No one's messing with me," I mumble, wishing Gee would go back to his movie.

Aubrey laughs. "I'm going to make her do it." I don't know why he sounds so sure.

"Can't make her," Gee says. "That's something she's gotta do on her own." He reaches for the remote and turns the volume up, as if we were the ones talking over his movie.

Aubrey pulls his phone out and his eyes get big. "Uh-oh," he says, "I better go." I thought I heard his phone buzzing a few times. I hope he's not in trouble for being at our house too long. He goes to find Mama to thank her for dinner, and then he walks out the front door without saying another thing to me.

If I was the type of person who could deliver a speech, I would maybe give a speech about the proper way to leave someone's house. Even if you have to rush home, saying goodbye before you leave is definitely rule number one.

30

GUNSHOTS

Used to be, Saturday mornings were magic.

Mama sleeps in on Saturdays, so even though in the afternoon she would have a whole list of chores for me, the morning was my time.

If I wanted, I could do absolutely no homework. Just lie in bed until ten and watch stuff on my laptop or count cracks in my ceiling.

Malcolm would get up, toss down some breakfast, and then spend hours outside, practicing his ball handling and taking a million shots. If I was feeling nice, I'd get up and rebound for him. But sometimes I'd pull the covers over my head and wish he would find something else to do on a Saturday morning.

That was before.

I didn't know how much I'd miss the *badoonk, badoonk* of the ball when Malcolm went away to college. I knew I'd miss *him*, but I didn't think I'd miss the noise, or the stinky uniforms in the laundry room, or his bad attitude after a loss. But I missed it all. Maybe because Malcolm *was* all those things. Like if we are all puzzles, then those were Malcolm's pieces.

And he's back, but there's no basketball. So what does Malcolm's puzzle look like now? What's he made of after I've taken such a big piece away?

Maybe it's silly of me to think that Rox could help piece Malcolm back together, but it's the only plan I have, so I reach over to my nightstand and grab my phone.

I missed you at the fish fry last night. Malcolm did too. He said so. And the shrimp was yummy!

Rox sends back a crying emoji face. Like she's real sad to have missed it.

That's a good sign. I nestle in my covers, trying to slide into the magic of a Saturday morning. I want to feel loose.

And I almost do it too. I snuggle into my cozy blankets and comfy pillow, letting worry and guilt slip off me like forgotten socks, but then loud bangs outside make me pop out of bed.

Were those *gun*shots? In our backyard?

I run out of my room and smack into Mama.

"Stay inside!" she hollers at me.

Malcolm's door opens, and he sticks his head out. "*What* is going on?"

"Watch Jenae!" Mama shouts at him as she bolts downstairs.

More gunfire pops, and then Mama's out the back door, and I hear her yelling but I can't make out what she's saying.

"Malcolm?" I ask my brother, my heart racing in my chest.

126

But he doesn't know what's going on either and just reaches back into his room for his crutches.

It doesn't take me more than a few seconds to make it downstairs, but it takes Malcolm longer, and I'm already at the French doors with my hand on the doorknob before Malcolm can catch me.

But his voice makes me stop.

"Jenae!" he hollers. "Hold *up*."

I stop, but that doesn't keep me from staring outside, my hand twisting the knob.

It's not hard to see the whole backyard. Not hard to see Mama shouting at Gee, who's got a tiny pistol in his hand. It's dull gray, and so small, it looks ridiculous in his big hand.

Mama tries to grab the gun from him, and everybody knows that's a bad idea.

Gee raises his hands and switches the gun from one hand to the other, while Mama tries to jump up and reach his hand. My heart thuds in my chest like cannonballs. What is he doing with a gun?

"What is *wrong* with him?" Malcolm says, pushing me out of the way and opening the door.

"He's going to shoot Mama!" I cry, following behind him.

Malcolm grabs me by the shoulder, as if he knew I was going to try and race outside. "No, he's not." His grip on my arm tightens. "Stay. In. Side." He gives my arm a shake, and his fingers are starting to pinch. I nod fast.

Then he crutches outside, leaving me all alone.

"Gee!" Malcolm shouts. "Hey, Gee!"

Mama yells at Malcolm to go back inside, but he ignores her. Gee looks at Malcolm, and then at Mama, and then up at the gun he's still holding above his head. His hand lowers, and with all my might I think, STOP!

And Gee crumples to the ground.

31

VITAL SIGNS

As soon as the ambulance leaves with Gee, I glide upstairs, quiet as a cloud. I go into my room and sit on my bed and rock back and forth.

I did it again.

Hurt someone without meaning to.

I didn't want Gee to fall down. All I wanted was for him not to shoot Mama.

The paramedics were like ants on sugar, all over Gee, putting a mask on his face and a needle in his arm and checking his vitals.

Hot tears streak down my face. Gee is vital to me. As vital as Mama and Malcolm. How could I have done that to him?

All I do is break things.

I climb into bed and pull the covers over my head and disappear.

I stay in bed all day. And when Malcolm knocks on my door and tells me to come eat something, I ignore him. I don't want anything. My pillow is wet, and I turn it over to the dry side.

And then I have to do that again. And again. I have a whole ocean inside me.

When I wake up in the morning, I force myself to go downstairs. Auntie Maug is in the kitchen with my uncle Harold. I don't see Uncle Harold that much because he lives all the way in the valley.

"Hey, Jenae," Auntie Maug says, her voice raspy and tired. She rubs a hand over her face. "Where do you all hide the coffee?"

Without answering her, I get the coffee from the freezer and measure out scoops into the coffeepot. I fill the reservoir with water and turn on the pot. I want to ask about Gee, but I'm too scared.

"Your grandpa had a stroke," Uncle Harold says. "A pretty big one. Doctors say he's had a whole bunch of small ones."

"Now, see, that just doesn't make sense to me," Auntie Maug says. "How they gonna tell us he's had all these strokes and we didn't know a thing about it?"

"I don't know, Maug," Uncle Harold says. "Guess it's common? And we saw how he's been getting confused lately."

"Thought it was just him getting old," Auntie Maug complains. "And him having his old gun? That was one of the strokes making him get that out?" She blows out a sharp burst of air.

"Why did he have a gun?" I ask, turning from the coffeepot.

Uncle Harold first says to Auntie Maug, "They don't know, Maug. Strokes can cause a lot of damage. Who knows what wires got crossed inside his head." Then he turns to me. "Your grandpa carried a gun when he delivered mail. Didn't like being

130

unprotected while he was walking around neighborhoods. Course, it would've gotten him fired if anyone had known. Ma used to have a fit about it. But I don't know what possessed him to get it out yesterday. Maybe he thought he was in one of those old Westerns, or I don't know, maybe he was getting ready to deliver mail like back in the day."

I blink slowly, afraid to ask what I really want to know. "Is he . . . is he . . . ?"

Auntie Maug comes over and squeezes my hand. "He regained consciousness once they got him to the hospital. They ran a whole bunch of tests, and they'll want to keep him a little longer, but he looked good after he came around, didn't he, Hal?" She looks over at her brother, sounding like she needs convincing.

I need convincing too, because I just can't believe that Gee is all right.

Monday morning, Gee isn't home from the hospital and Mama tells Malcolm to take me to school. I don't want to go, but Mama's not having it. You basically have to be bleeding to death for Mama to say it's okay to miss a day of school. And she waves away my questions about Gee like I'm a pesky fly.

I ride in Malcolm's car pressed against the door, wishing we were driving to the hospital instead of school. Mama said I'm too young to get to visit Gee, and that doesn't seem fair. I need to see him. I need to tell him how sorry I am.

When we pull up to the school, Malcolm points to a banner

that someone put up. The banner reads SYLVIA MENDEZ JUNIOR HIGH, and it's covering the John Wayne sign.

"Folks sure are doing the most over this thing."

I just shrug, not caring. I climb out of the car and slide into invisibility like it's a pool of water. I don't make a single ripple.

I feel Aubrey trying to see me. Staring at my chair. Tapping my desk. But I dissolve into the hard gray plastic of my seat. Mrs. Crawford doesn't call on me.

At lunch, I whisk down a hallway, and then another, and end up in a room with a stage and a small curtain.

Stars are painted on the floor instead of the ceiling, and I lie down in that field of stars and let myself melt into the dark sky.

"Jenae, what's the matter? What are you doing?"

Red fire. I turn away.

"You didn't go to our lunch spot. You came here instead."

Why is Aubrey telling me things I know? Why can't he leave me alone? I press hard into the floor. I throw a flood of thoughts at him. *GO AWAY! LEAVE ME ALONE! GO! GO!*

Aubrey comes closer. "Jenae? What is it?"

With a sigh that comes from my toes, I sit up. "What do you want?"

"I was worried. Are you okay?"

I'm not okay. But what's wrong with me isn't the type of thing you can say. I hurt my brother. I hurt my grandfather. And I did both even though I already knew what I could do. How I could mess things up. I am the worst type of person who ever lived.

"I'm fine," I whisper; the words are spiderwebs. Frail and sticky.

A harsh light comes on. "You kids can't be in here at lunch," a voice says. The drama teacher. Ms. Lee. She walks over to us. "Is everything okay?"

I rub my face, erasing the wet trails, and look at my shoes.

"Sorry!" Aubrey says, working his smile. "We were just practicing for a speech we have to give."

Mama told me never trust someone who spills lies like tea, but I can't be mad at Aubrey for lying to save us.

Ms. Lee steps forward until she's all the way at the edge of the low stage. She squats down and looks at me. "Is that what was going on here?" she asks me.

I think about how it might look. Two kids in a dark room with no adults around. I nod solemnly at her.

"Well, this isn't really where you should be practicing," Ms. Lee says. She doesn't sound angry. Her voice is soft, and I think maybe if I told her what I did to Gee, she'd let me stay here.

"Sorry," Aubrey says again.

I don't answer, but I pull myself off the floor, even though I just want to stay there, lying in the stars.

32

COMPLETELY IMPOSSIBLE

"Come on," Aubrey says. "Lunch is going to be over soon. Let's at least get some air for a minute."

He leads me outside, and I'm not sure how. He's not pulling on me, or pushing me, but my steps follow his.

Outside he looks at me hard. "What happened?" he asks. "Something happened, right?"

Instead of answering him, I reach up and touch his hair. It's soft like the baby lambs at the petting zoo.

"Why do you dye your hair?" I ask, not expecting him to answer me.

Aubrey swallows once, twice. He rubs his hand over his hair, like he could wipe the color off. Then he takes a tiny piece and starts twisting. "I had leukemia. Cancer. When I was a kid. Chemo made me lose my hair." He sounds like he's reciting a grocery list. As if none of it is important. "My mom said once my hair grew back I could do anything I wanted with it. Cut it. Dye it. Let it grow into a super-big Afro. Anything.

I had a Mohawk for a while. This year I decided to dye it red."

I'm so shocked, I don't know what to say. I feel like I should apologize, but I don't know for what exactly. We did a fundraiser in fourth grade to raise money to help kids with cancer. The stories were sad, and pretty much everyone brought whatever they had in their piggy banks to help. I felt so bad for those kids, but Aubrey is standing right here in front of me, looking healthy and not a bit sick.

"Are you okay now?" I ask, and then I look at the floor, worried about the answer.

"I'm *fine*," he says, and then he narrows his eyes at me. "So what happened to you?"

I twist the end of my ponytail, hoping it will work for me like it works for Aubrey. Instead, I feel worse. Like I'm on a stage. With a hot spotlight shining in my face. "My grandfather had a stroke. I made him have it. Just like I made my brother get hurt playing basketball, and I—" I stop quick because I can't admit to the other thing. "I hurt them both. Because I wanted my brother home, and I wanted Gee to put down the gun."

Aubrey's eyes don't get big until I say the word *gun*.

My chest goes up and down so hard it hurts. I can't catch my breath.

"Jenae," Aubrey says, speaking slowly; it must be hard for him. "You can't control stuff like that."

"You don't know," I tell him. "You don't."

"I know it's completely impossible," Aubrey says. "You

didn't make those things happen. That's quack!" His voice is getting ramped up . . . and loud.

"It doesn't matter if you don't believe me, Aubrey. I know what I know."

"You can't *know* something like that!" he shouts at me.

I shake my head at Aubrey. There's no use trying to explain something that sounds impossible.

"Okay, make me do something," he says. "Anything. Something small." He puts his hands on his hips, waiting, staring hard at me.

"I can't," I say. My fingers twist together, and I try to slow my breathing. I don't know how to make him understand. "I think it only works when I'm really upset," I mumble.

"You really believe this?" Aubrey's golden eyes search my face as if he's waiting for me to shout out, *Gotchu!* As if it all might be some big joke.

But I just nod slowly. Just because it sounds ridiculous doesn't make it untrue. I gulp down the tears that want to spill out, and ocean saltiness burns my throat.

The bell rings.

"Come on, let's get to class," Aubrey says.

My feet follow Aubrey's.

In English, Mr. Humphries rubs his hands together like something exciting is going to happen. "I thought we could limber up our minds by giving impromptu speeches on the reading from Friday." He seems to be looking right at me. "The more you practice speaking in front of people, the easier it will get."

I will not a give a speech today. *NO. I WILL NOT GIVE A SPEECH TODAY. NO! NO!* I shout it over and over in my head. I'm concentrating so hard, I think I might pass out.

33

A LITTLE INVISIBLE

Mr. Humphries steps around his desk.

"You know, the more I think about it, I'd rather have you write up your thoughts," he says. "I want you to really think about *Coraline* and how some of her decision-making might mirror your own." Mr. Humphries pauses, and for a minute he looks confused, like he was reading a book and accidentally skipped a page.

I look back at Aubrey. Now he knows. That's what I can do.

For the rest of the period I watch my hand write line after line of thoughts about a girl whose mother has button eyes. A girl who is, sometimes, a little invisible.

I think about mice. And spiders. And Malcolm. And Gee. And my dad. And wanting something too much.

When the bell rings, it makes me jump. I quickly gather my things together so I can get to my last period, but when I get out into the hallway, Aubrey grabs my arm.

"You did *not* make Mr. Humphries not assign a speech," he whispers. Well, *tries* to whisper, but he's so aggravated his voice is husky but loud, and a few people glance over at us.

I guess this is what being friends with someone means. Them knowing what you're thinking before you've said a word.

"How do you know?" I ask.

"Jenae!"

"I have to get to class," I say as I pull away.

I've done awful things with my mind, and being sorry doesn't cut it, but making Mr. Humphries change his mind about us giving speeches today? I'm not sorry about that at all.

But I am sorry that Aubrey is right in front of school when I come out at the end of the day. Of course he wants to try and convince me I don't know what I know. I don't want to listen.

"I gotta go," I say, and start walking down the street.

Aubrey just follows me. "Jenae," he says, his voice serious and low. "You need to quit."

I stop and face him. "You were *there*. You saw Mr. Humphries getting ready to assign a speech and then decide not to. And he didn't know why."

"People change their minds all the time."

It's hot, and I feel my feet starting to melt into the sidewalk. I notice the Sylvia Mendez banner is gone. I wonder if the people on the corner with John Wayne signs took it down or if it was our principal. I wipe the sweat off the back of my neck.

"I'm sorry."

"Sorry for what?" Aubrey asks, scrunching his eyebrows together in confusion.

"About your cancer," I say softly, not sure how I should say it. I look at him and then look at the ground.

"That's a quack thing to be sorry for."

I can't tell by Aubrey's voice if he's annoyed. I look up, and he's smiling at me.

I nod at him, because maybe he's right, and then I turn away and start walking down the street again.

Aubrey keeps walking next to me, even though he should know I don't want company right now. We walk half a block without either of us saying anything. Then he says, "So you made your brother's knee get messed up and you made your grandfather have a stroke. And you made Mr. Humphries not assign a speech today. Is that it? With your superpower, haven't you done a bunch more?"

I don't want to answer that question. I haven't done a *bunch* more, but I did one other thing. A very bad thing.

34

THE WORST PERSON EVER

When I was little, all I wanted was for Mama and my dad to stay together—for us to be complete. But my parents fought *all* the time. We didn't live with Gee then. We had a small house that made it really easy to hear all the fighting. Their fights made our house feel wrong. Like it had a bad attitude. One night it got so bad, I aimed one thought at my dad as hard as I could. Telling him, *JUST GO.* And he did. At first, Mama seemed happy, and I thought I had done a good thing. But then she got so sad. With one thought, I made my dad leave and broke Mama's heart. And I couldn't take it back. No matter how much I begged the universe. All I could do was become as small and quiet as I could be and try as hard as I could not to make anything else bad happen. But I did anyway.

"No," I say so quietly, I'm not sure if Aubrey heard me.

Then I say, "It doesn't matter. I just have to stop." I take a step away from him, but he grabs my arm.

When I look at his hand, he quickly lets go.

"You know Astrid Dane is fantasy, right?" he asks. "It's not real? Stuff like that, magical stuff, can't really happen."

"I'm not dumb," I say, even though that's exactly how I feel. I don't know how to explain that magic, *real* magic, isn't real, but this is.

"I know you're not," he says, sounding like he feels sorry for me. Then his wide grin is back, and I can tell he is ready to change the subject. Me too.

"Hey, you know what?" He takes his cell phone out of his back pocket. "We should exchange numbers. In case, you know, something happens again and you want to tell me?"

"Okay," I say slowly. I didn't know it was possible to feel good and bad at the same time. Us having each other's numbers feels like it settles the friendship question, but I can't help thinking about the persuasive speech and how I'm plotting to get out of it. I hate the idea of giving Aubrey my phone number when he's probably going to want to delete it soon. Still, I tell him my number.

He taps away, and then he gives me a small smile. "I texted you mine," he says.

I feel my phone vibrate in my bag, but I don't pull it out.

We start walking down the street again, and the sun feels good on my face and both of our Astrid Dane bags are swinging back and forth, and I'm feeling like having a friend is something I could get used to, when I remember I don't deserve one speck of happiness. Not an atom's worth. Not a neutron or neuron or whatever it is that's smaller than an atom.

I stop again. I shift over on the sidewalk so other people walking home from school can pass by. "You probably shouldn't come over today."

"Why not?" Aubrey asks me, and he sounds so curious, as if he can't think of any possible reason for him not to come over. He shifts his bag from one shoulder to the other.

It's sort of irritating for someone to think they should be able to go anywhere or do anything. That they're just welcome every single place.

"Because I don't want you to," I say. And I don't want to sound mean and angry, but I know that's exactly how I sound. And I can't tell Aubrey it's because even though he doesn't believe I'm the worst person ever, he's going to soon.

Aubrey looks at me hard and tilts his head the way a dog does when it's trying to figure something out, and then he nods and says, "Got it."

I nod back with a hard snap of my head and then turn stiffly on my heel and start down the street, knowing he's watching me, knowing if I turn around and say, *Never mind, come on*, he'll be right there. I pick my feet up faster and let myself get swallowed up in the stream of people.

If Aubrey came to my house with me, we could watch Astrid Dane videos and get started on homework. As much as I fought against it, having a friend, having Aubrey, has been nice. Better than nice. And maybe, maybe, no matter what I've done, I do deserve that one small thing.

I turn around, expecting Aubrey to be there. Expecting him to know me well enough to have snuck behind me like he did before and be standing there with that mile-wide grin pasted across his face.

But he's not.

35

CAN'T OR WON'T

My feet drag along the sidewalk, and my bag bumps annoyingly into my hip.

The house feels lonely when I get home. No Western movie blasting on the TV, no music coming from Malcolm's room. I kick off my shoes and think about leaving them right there in the middle of the living room, but then think better of it and carry them up to my room.

I sit on my bed, letting grumpiness crawl all over me. Nothing seems fair.

I fall back on my bed and stare at the ceiling. There's a crack in the plaster that looks like lightning. Gee's had it plastered over a few times, but it always comes right back. *Old is like that,* Gee says. *Determined.* Gee made it seem as if old was a good thing, but how good is old, if it makes it easy for you to have a stroke?

"I didn't mean it," I whisper. I roll over and grab an Astrid Dane graphic novel from my bookcase. But after flipping through a few pages, even that doesn't make me feel better.

Then I hear the front door open and close, and I rush out to the stair landing, hoping I'll see Gee coming through the door, but it's just Mama. It's too early for her to be home from work, and my legs get wobbly.

"Mama?" I ask, my voice as shaky as my legs. "Is everything okay?"

Mama looks up at me, and her face is full of worry, but then she gives me a half smile. "Yeah, everything's fine."

I don't believe her. "Did something happen?" I want to rush downstairs and get closer to her, but I'm afraid.

"Is Gee . . . ?" I can't make myself ask.

"I don't know, Jenae," she says, and then I guess she realizes how that sounds because she quickly adds, "He's okay. I mean he's still at the hospital, but I think they'll release him soon. The doctors say—" She snaps her fingers and points to the spot in front of her. "Girl, can you come down here? I'm getting a crick in my neck staring up these stairs."

"What do the doctors say?" I ask as I come down the stairs.

She doesn't answer until I'm right in front of her. "He's not talking. And they don't know why. Strokes can affect speech, but this seems strange to them. That's why they've been keeping him. Trying to find out what's going on."

"He can't talk?"

She shakes her head. "They don't know. He's not trying to say anything. So they don't know if he can't or won't."

"What do you mean, *won't*?" I think of Gee and how he

loves telling me stories about back in the day. How he teases me and Mama and anybody else nearby.

Mama rubs her temples. "I'm talking plain English, Jenae— what exactly do you not understand? Won't. Will *not*." She glances up the stairs. "Where's your brother?"

I shrug. "He wasn't here when I got home." Malcolm's been pretty sour the last few days. Before Gee's stroke, he seemed like he was getting better, or at least he seemed less angry, and I had begun to think my plan was working. I was sure my texts to Rox had gotten her to get in touch with Malcolm. But I haven't texted her since Gee's stroke. Maybe Malcolm is sad about Gee like I am, but maybe he's bothered that he hasn't heard from Rox. I better text her again.

"This boy," Mama mutters as she heads to the kitchen.

"Mama," I say, following her, "how will they know? Whether Gee can't or—" My question doesn't make it past my lips because Mama is just standing in the kitchen staring out the window, looking so down it makes me worry she's about to start crying.

"Mama?" I whisper, scared that she must not have told me the truth about Gee and he's really so much worse.

Mama doesn't answer right away, but then she pats her hair as if a few strands have gotten out of place and gives me a half-hearted smile. She gets iced tea out of the fridge and nods at it to ask if I want a glass, but I shake my head. After she takes a good long sip, she says, "Coach Naz, one of your brother's assistant coaches? Has been calling me every few days to check in, but today the head coach called. Coach Julius. Since Malcolm hasn't registered for fall quarter, they're thinking he doesn't plan on coming back. And if he doesn't . . . he'll for sure lose his scholarship. The quarter is about to start." Her fingers grip so tight around her glass, I worry she might crack it.

"It'll be okay, Mama," I say fast, even though I don't know if that's true.

"Humph," she says, like I don't know a thing. Then she walks over to the sink and pours out the rest of her tea. She leans back against the counter, and it's as if she's just now seeing me. "Did you even brush your hair today?"

My hands fly to my head, trying to smooth the wild wisps of hair snaking around my head. I actually don't think I did, but I say, "*Yes*, Mama."

Mama sighs and shakes her head. "You really don't care, do you?"

I care about so many things. Maybe too many, and maybe too much, but the things I care about Mama would say don't matter. And the things she *wants* me to care about I just don't get. I wish I could make her see me as I am instead of what I'm not.

36
BATTLE SCARS

I text Rox before I start my homework.

Gee had a stroke. And Malcolm is so grumpy again. He said he wished you two were close like you used to be. He needs someone to talk to. We're both scared about Gee.

Rox texts me back a few minutes later.

Oh no. I always loved your grandpa. Is he all right?

I don't know.

I hear the front door close downstairs, and I almost drop my phone. It must be Malcolm getting back, and I feel as if he's caught me texting Rox, even though I know that's silly. I quickly text:

Will you talk to Malcolm?

I'm not sure if I'm really the person he wants to talk to. He hurt me so I hurt him and now it might be too late.

I feel bad for a second because maybe Rox is right. Maybe

Malcolm really doesn't want to hear from her. But I can't risk letting go of my plan.

It's not too late. Before Gee's stroke he was talking about you and his voice was all smiley. He said he wished things hadn't gotten so messed up. I know he wants to call you but he's afraid.

I bite my lip hard after texting that. Saying Malcolm is afraid feels like I pushed him outside naked.

If you're sure it won't make him mad. I'll ask him if he wants to get together.

Yay! But don't tell him I told you anything. He'd be embarrassed.

Got it.

With a relieved sigh, I shove my phone under my pillow and finish up my homework.

When I head downstairs a little while later, I find Malcolm on the couch. His knee-bender machine is next to him, but he's not using it.

He repositions himself, making room for me. He's wearing shorts, and without his brace, I can see the big scar slashed across his knee. It's raised and darker than his skin. It makes him look like a warrior.

"Where were you earlier?" I ask, hoping he might have been at PT.

He frowns, and I expect him to say I'm not the boss of him

and it's none of my business, but instead he says, "Just driving around. Needed to get out of the house."

That doesn't sound so bad. Gee says getting out in the world can make a problem seem smaller. But it doesn't seem like Malcolm's drive helped him at all.

I can't help staring at his scar, which is maybe why he grabs his knee brace and straps it on. Scars don't bother me. Lots of people have scars. But even though I think it makes him look like he survived a battle, I wish I hadn't caused Malcolm's.

"Malcolm," I say, so softly he doesn't even look toward me. "I missed you when you left for school. It was lonely." My chest aches, and it feels as if my heart is too big. Like with each heavy beat it gets bigger and bigger, and in a moment, it might burst. "But . . . I never wanted you to get hurt."

He hears that last part. Instead of him looking at me like he understands and appreciates me saying that to him, his face gets angry. "Tell me something I don't know." He scowls, and I wonder just how mad he'd get if I were to tell him what he doesn't know. That I wanted him back home so much, I made him get hurt.

"Maybe the next time you go driving around, you could, um, catch up with old friends or something?" I don't want to come right out and say he should go see Rox, but I'm laying the groundwork, which is pretty ironic, because it's something Mr. Humphries said we should do when we are making a good argument. *Laying the groundwork*, he said, *starts establishing the direction you're going to go.*

"Hah! Nobody I feel like catching up with," Malcolm says.

Then he slowly gets up, grabs his crutches, and makes his way to the stairs. Before he starts up, he sighs so loud it's like he's trying to get something unstuck from his throat. Then he starts hopping.

How mad will Malcolm be if he finds out about me talking to Rox about him? I picture Malcolm's face. His really, really mad one. His eyes so angry they are just tiny slits of fury.

Malcolm stops midway up the stairs. Going up steps with a busted knee is hard. I can hear him panting all the way from here. Then he starts again and finally makes it to the top. After a few seconds, his door opens and closes, and then music starts thumping.

The hard beats are like angry thunderclaps. I wonder what bothers Malcolm more, not playing basketball or being back home with us? He and I used to play Sorry! all the time, and he'd get so mad whenever he got one of those move-backward cards. Maybe that's how he feels now. Like he got dealt the worst card ever.

As much as I've been focused on fixing Malcolm, I haven't thought too much about what that means. I want him to be happier. And Rox can probably help with that, but really what would make him the happiest is being able to play ball again. Not just play, but be as good as he used to be, and play for his team. That means him going away again. But could he maybe be happy without basketball? Is it so bad being home with me?

37

ONLY PERSON IN THE WORLD

Mama and I don't talk much on our way to school in the morning. I guess she's too worried about Gee to be bothering with
me, and I'm too worried about everything, especially what I'm
going to say to Aubrey when I see him. Maybe I should've texted him, telling him I was sorry for being sort of rude about
him coming over.

When I scan the crowd of people in front of the school, I
see Tía Rosalie right in the midst of it, holding a sign that says
SAY YES TO CHANGE.

She notices me going up the steps of the school and waves. I
wave back but don't stop to say hi—I'm too worried about what
I'm going to say when I see Aubrey.

But worrying was a waste of time, because Aubrey's not at
his desk in history, and he doesn't come rushing in late. He's just
absent.

I know it's silly, but I can't help thinking that him not being
there has something to do with me. That he couldn't stand the

thought of sitting next to me in class because I got angry at him yesterday.

By the time lunch rolls around, I've convinced myself that either Aubrey hates me or his cancer came back last night and he had to be rushed to the hospital. I sit by myself at lunch, imagining him pale faced in a hospital bed, looking strangely like Gee, and coughing and trying to tell his mother that he needs to talk to his friend Jenae one last time.

Fat tears drip all over my Brie and fig jam, and I'm seriously considering calling Mama to pick me up so we can go check hospitals.

I shove my half-eaten lunch back into my bag and stare across the field at the whole world of people eating and laughing and gossiping and running and playing catch. Not one of them knows me. Not one of them sees me. What are they talking about? What do they care about? Are any of them friends with Aubrey? Do they know where he is? It's just a wide stretch of grass between me and them, but it seems like a lot more.

I don't fit in there, but maybe Aubrey doesn't either. Maybe that's why we fit together pretty well. And now he's gone.

My stress sweat picks up, and I hop to my feet. Where is he? What happened?

I stare hard across the field, wondering what Astrid Dane would do. How would she get information, or maybe just escape from the prison of school, or whatever it is I have to do to find Aubrey? I pull my phone out, not sure what I'm going to do with it. Text him? Call hospitals? And then I see it.

Flaming-hot-Cheeto hair. Right in the midst of the lunch area. Hair that is quite obviously not resting on a hospital pillow.

I march across the field and stomp my way in front of Aubrey. My chest heaves up and down, and my breath comes out in hard, choppy wheezes. He is standing at the edge of a lunch table, not really with the laughing group of eighth graders, just near them. But I don't stop to think about that. I'm too mad.

"What happened to you?" I demand, so furious at him that the words spit from my mouth. "I thought—I thought . . ."

Aubrey stares at me, shocked. The table full of people stare. At me.

Heat engulfs my whole head, threatening to consume me. I try to sink into the asphalt. Try to make my body liquid so it can become a puddle that will slowly evaporate.

"Jenae?" Aubrey asks, as if he isn't sure it's really me.

It most definitely is not really me. All around the lunch area, I can feel eyes turning my way. Looking at me. Wondering about me. I want to disappear. I try to make myself invisible, but it doesn't work.

"I was scared," I whisper, and then I turn away from him and run.

You might think a chubby girl wouldn't be very fast, but I am lightning. I am a bullet train. A shooting star. I am the Flash. I hear Aubrey calling me for only a second before there is no sound except the sonic wind blowing past me.

I run so fast, I make it all the way back to an alternate

universe. One where I am invisible Jenae. With a healthy grandfather and a brother who has just left for college and will blow everyone's mind with how awesome he is. I press my back against a building, feeling every dimple of the stuccoed wall. I press back even harder and almost convince myself that the building will absorb me and let me become a part of it. It feels good. It feels right. For the whole time I am panting and mopping sweat off my forehead, I think I have figured out my entire future. I am a wall. I can disappear and become stucco. My breathing slows down.

It occurs to me that although it was starting to feel like I had known Aubrey for ages, we actually just met, and I don't know him at all. Not really. And that maybe, when I pushed him away for like the hundredth time, he decided I really didn't want to be friends. *If you ask for space often enough*, Gee once told me, *folks sure enough are going to give it to you.*

Maybe, just maybe, I am the most ridiculous person who has ever lived.

I push off the wall. Because who wants to be part of a building? Especially a *school* building? Staring at loud, rude, farting, and burping kids all day long?

38

BIG ENOUGH

In English, before I take my seat, I look at Aubrey, waiting for him to meet my eyes. When he finally does, I beam a thought hard at him. The thought is in bold type, and underlined and in all caps. It is so loud, I'm sure the whole class can hear it. *I WANT TO BE FRIENDS.*

His smile spreads so wide I'm surprised his cheeks don't crack.

"Listen up," Mr. Humphries says, calling the class to attention. "There are a lot of steps involved with making an effective argument. One key thing for you to do is research. Not only will learning how to research aid you with your topics, it will also help with papers you'll write in high school and college. It's important to know how to get information that's accurate and how to make use of it without just copying what you read. So we're going to head to the library to explore the glories of research."

Not for the first time, I think how strange Mr. Humphries is.

Aubrey falls in line next to me, and even though we don't say anything to each other, it feels like we are connected.

I haven't been to the school library before. It was locked when Malcolm gave me the tour. Our elementary school library was tiny, and the nonfiction part was much bigger than the fiction section. But John Wayne Junior High has a big library, with windows lining up one wall letting in lots of light. There's rows and rows of fiction, and I wish we were there to check out books instead of doing research for a speech I know I can't do. A painting of John Wayne covers one wall. He is wearing a cowboy hat and a wide smile, like he's thinking, *Come on in—welcome to my library!* I sure hope he'd be saying that to every student, no matter what they look like.

Mr. Humphries leads us to a big bank of computers, and the librarian, Ms. Kompos, comes over to meet us. She seems really friendly.

She explains a few rules to us, and then Mr. Humphries tells the class to get with our partners at a computer. He'll come around and check on us.

Before I can say anything to Aubrey, he whispers to me, "Why were you worried about me?"

I gulp before asking, "Can the cancer, the leukemia, can it come back? Can you get sick again?" I say a silent prayer for the answer I want.

Aubrey is really fair, but sometimes, like right now, it seems like even the little bit of color he has fades away and he just becomes a blank space of freckles.

He starts typing on the computer, and I worry he's not going to answer me. Then he turns the screen toward me. There's lots of results all about childhood leukemia and survival rates and how if it's been over five years, chances are better that the cancer won't come back. It's not 100 percent or anything, but enough that I feel my heart go back to thumping at a regular rhythm.

"That's what you were worried about?" Aubrey whispers. "Just because I wasn't in first period?"

I nod. "And you weren't at lunch." My eyes tighten. "At least I thought you weren't."

Aubrey twists a tiny section of hair and sighs. It's weird seeing him look so serious. "Look, I get checked every year."

Mr. Humphries starts heading toward us, and Aubrey quickly types in *Sylvia Mendez* so it looks like we're doing what we're supposed to. Before getting to us, Mr. Humphries stops at Sophia and Rose's computer and starts pointing out something to them.

"My doctor in Chicago was always really positive that I'm one of the lucky ones," Aubrey whispers. "And my new doctor here agrees. So you don't need to worry."

I glance back at the computer screen. I wish it was 100 percent. "I can't help it."

"I'm surprised you were worried," Aubrey says. "The reason I didn't sit with you at lunch is because sometimes it seems like you don't want me around." He rubs a hand over his head. "You can just tell me if you don't." He doesn't look at me.

I shake my head and say, "Yesterday was just a bad day."

"Okay, well, we can't be friends if you're going to be worried every second that I'm going to get sick again." He still isn't looking at me. As if he's afraid of what he might see in my eyes.

Would he really not want to be friends just because I worried about him? That doesn't seem right. Shouldn't a friend worry?

"It's why I didn't tell you." He blinks a bunch of times, and I want to ask him if his friends in Chicago never worried about the cancer coming back. Maybe they worried and just didn't tell him.

I've always assumed a friend is who you tell everything to, and I'm just about to tell Aubrey that when Mr. Humphries walks up behind us. "So, what's your topic?"

When we tell him the school name change, he gets a big grin. "I'm glad one of the groups in class is tackling that issue," he says. "It might not seem like it affects you much, but it's important to look at both sides. How much have you learned so far?"

I'm glad Gee had me look up information about Sylvia Mendez, because I'm able to tell Mr. Humphries about Sylvia's parents wanting her to go to the school that was close to their house. And how the superintendent of the district said terrible things about Mexicans when he testified at the trial.

"Sounds like you've been doing your research," Mr. Humphries says, nodding. "And why do you think *this* school is the one being considered? Why not the school she went to?" Mr. Humphries doesn't pause to let us answer him, which is good, because I don't know the answers to those questions. "And what about the other side?" he asks. "This is a two-sided speech. What's important about John Wayne? Why was the school named after him in the first place? If there was a good reason to name the school John Wayne, are things different now?"

I look at John Wayne's picture. A smile that wide should be big enough to include everybody.

Aubrey doesn't say anything, but I can tell from his eyes all sorts of thoughts are buzzing around in his head.

Mr. Humphries steps to the next set of partners and starts asking them questions about their topic.

It makes me feel a little sick that someone who thought it was okay to say horrible things about people of other races deserves to be honored. Hopefully when they decided to name our school after John Wayne, he was just the good guy in the Westerns who always saved the day and knew for sure what was right and what was wrong.

I think about Mr. Humphries's question about why *our* school. Even though people in our neighborhood don't all look the same, you hear a lot of Spanish when you're walking down the streets.

Sylvia probably would've felt welcome at our school. It would be cool if kids in this neighborhood could go to a school that told them they belonged.

After making his way around to each group, Mr. Humphries has us all stop researching. "You're all making good progress. Make sure you find facts to develop your argument, but also try to find information for the side you're not supporting.

Knowing both sides will always make your argument stronger. If any of you have trouble accessing a computer or using the public library, please let me know. I want to make sure you all have an equal opportunity to give great speeches." He smiles.

The word *speeches* makes my mouth go dry, and my stress sweat starts pinging out all over. Doing research is interesting and almost fun; giving a speech is the opposite of that. No way. I can't. I push away from the desk, away from the computer, away from Aubrey.

"It'll be okay," Aubrey whispers, as if he knows exactly what I'm thinking.

"I can't wait to see which seventh graders will be joining us in the debate club," Mr. Humphries says. "The first group of partners will go this coming Monday. Who wants to volunteer?" A few hands spring up. I stare hard at Aubrey's hands, forcing them to stay down. I think if he tried to raise one, I'd chop it off.

Looking right at me, Mr. Humphries says, "Sometimes it's good to just get something you're afraid of doing over with. Then you can stop worrying about it."

People say the same thing about yanking out a loose tooth. Well, pulling a wobbly tooth hurts like nobody's business. No, thanks.

"I don't want these speeches to eat up a whole week, so no makeups. Monday, Tuesday, Wednesday. That's what you have." Mr. Humphries still seems to be looking at me.

After class, Aubrey says, "Just watch, Jenae! We're going to be the best, and once we're in the club, you'll see it's fun doing debates!"

He must see the look of horror on my face, because he says, "Don't worry. It'll be okay. We don't have to go Monday. Or even Tuesday. We can be the last ones if you want."

I don't want. Not any part of it. It's too late for me to tell Aubrey he needs to find a new partner. Everyone else has already been partnered up, so he's stuck with me.

"I can come over and we can practice," he says.

"No," I say, probably too fast. "I mean . . ." Why does Aubrey have to be so excited about debate club anyway? Isn't that the same as him saying being friends with me isn't enough? "It's not a good day for company."

Aubrey seems disappointed, but I don't think there's anything I can do to change that. Besides, I didn't really lie. Aubrey is like lightning. He's bright and has so much flash and energy. It doesn't seem right bringing that home right now.

"See ya," I say, and head to sixth period.

39

BACK TO INVISIBLE

In math, I relax into numbers, and for forty-five minutes, things make sense.

After school, I'm grateful there's no sign of Aubrey, because I don't want to talk about our speeches. With the people in front of the school waving signs and chanting about history and John Wayne and Sylvia Mendez, it would've been hard to avoid. People honk their horns as they drive by, but there's no way to tell if they're honking for or against the name change.

I walk quickly past the line of people, keeping my head down, hoping I won't see Tía Rosalie and anxious to get out of the commotion.

Mr. Humphries saying there won't be time for makeups was perfect. Now I don't have to worry Mr. Humphries would just have Aubrey and me go on a different day when I don't show up.

That's my plan. I'm going to have my dad get me out of school Wednesday—the day Aubrey signed us up to go. The last day possible.

My dad has told me a bunch of times he'll do anything

for me. I've never tested him before. My head hurts worrying about it.

When I'm not there, Aubrey will be so mad, and he's not going to forgive me.

And I guess I will go back to invisible Jenae. For some reason, that doesn't sound as appealing as it used to.

But when I get home, I don't have time to worry about speeches or Aubrey or anything else, because Gee is home. The television is blaring, and he has a blanket over him like it's the middle of the winter.

Malcolm has a chair pulled up next to Gee, and he's eating sunflower seeds.

"Gee!" I call out, and rush to his side. He doesn't answer me, so I pick up his hand and squeeze it. His skin feels paper-thin, and I can't remember if it felt that way before he went to the hospital.

"How are you feeling?" I ask, setting down his hand and giving a light feather touch to his blanket. It's one of those throws people like to give for Christmas when they don't know you very well.

Gee still doesn't answer me, and I think about what Mama said.

"Hello to you too," Malcolm teases.

"Hey, Malcolm," I say, not taking my eyes off Gee. "Is Gee . . . ?" I lean away from Gee, closer to my brother, so I can whisper. "Is he still not talking?"

Malcolm gives Gee's shoulder a small push. "Whatcha think, Gee? You got something to say?"

Gee turns his head, slow, slow, slow, and considers Malcolm before turning back to his movie.

"Cool with me, old man," Malcolm says. "I don't even blame you. People talk too much." Malcolm points to a notepad next to Gee that I hadn't noticed. "Mama put that out. Said Gee could write down anything he wants to say, but he doesn't seem interested." He relaxes back into his chair and tosses more seeds into his mouth. A pile of shells is on a paper towel next to him. I like sunflower seeds, but I don't like the mess of shells they leave behind.

"Where is Mama?" I ask.

"She had to go back to work after she brought Gee home. Some big project or something."

"But . . ." I want to say that somebody should be here taking care of Gee. Somebody who isn't broken too.

"Aw, look, Gee! The dude is hiding in the canyon," Malcolm says, like Westerns are suddenly his favorite thing too, and it doesn't seem like there's space for me.

I head to the kitchen to make myself a snack. Before I go through the swinging door, I look back at Gee and Malcolm.

Out of all the people in the world I could've hurt, I hurt the only two people who think I'm fine just the way I am. I push the door hard and rush past before it can whack me.

Suddenly, a snack doesn't sound so good. I want to scream and shout. I want to tell everybody that the worst girl in the world lives right here in this house. Instead, I pour Malcolm and Gee each a glass of iced tea and even put a sprig of mint in their glasses.

I head back into the living room and hand Malcolm his, but when I try to hand Gee his glass, Malcolm waves it away. "He's good for now." I set the glass next to Gee in case he wants it later, then settle on the couch. I should probably start on homework, but for now I just want to sit behind Malcolm and Gee, concentrating on them both as hard as I can.

Malcolm keeps talking to Gee, even though Gee isn't saying a word.

"Oh, man, Gee, didn't I tell you the dude was going to get caught on purpose? Bet you didn't see that coming."

Mama told me once that when Malcolm was little, he'd sit on Gee's lap and the two of them would watch Westerns together. Watching the two of them now I can completely see it. Small Malcolm, not even aware there was something called basketball yet, cuddled up in Gee's lap, feeling a steady beating heart and strong arms.

If I let the couch swallow me whole and disappear entirely, I'm certain both Gee and Malcolm wouldn't notice.

I clear my throat. "Do you like this one, Gee? Is John Wayne in it?"

"Me and Gee are done with John Wayne," Malcolm says, tipping his glass at Gee. "Plenty of Westerns that don't have his racist butt starring in them."

I don't think Gee has decided any such thing; I'm sure

Malcolm has made this decision for both of them, and that doesn't seem fair.

"If he was so racist, why do some people want the school to stay named after him?"

Malcolm cracks a mouthful of seeds before answering me. "That's a good question. Why would they?"

"Because they don't think he was racist?"

Malcolm shakes his head.

"Because they don't like change? That makes the most sense to me." I've been thinking about this a lot. Even if Mr. Humphries hadn't told us that it's a good idea to look at the other side when figuring out your argument. The people I saw outside the school who want the school to stay John Wayne don't seem bad or mean. "Lots of people don't like change."

Malcolm says, "I think it's more than that." He cracks some more seeds in his mouth. "But you're right about change. I don't know why people are always on hype about change being good."

I don't think he's thinking about my school; he's probably thinking about how his life has changed. I try to think of something to say, so even though I'm one of those people who don't particularly like change, I say, "Well, but sometimes, even when we don't see it at first"—I pause because I feel like I have to be really careful so I don't make Malcolm mad—"maybe even a bad change can work out okay in the end?" The last few words come out a little breathless, like I was running a race.

Malcolm frowns at me. Then he points at his knee. "This is

going to be good? How? Tell me how, Jenae." His voice is raised and angry, and a tremor runs through Gee, and I can't tell if he is shaking his head or just trembling.

When I don't answer him, Malcolm gets up and starts the long journey upstairs, leaving his mess of seeds behind.

After his door slams shut, I look at the ceiling and imagine Malcolm up in his room, being angry and disappointed. I pull my phone out and stare at Rox's name. She said she was going to call him. Why hasn't she?

Malcolm isn't doing so good.

It's not an awful message. Not really. It's just the truth. So why do I feel so bad when I press send?

40
GOING SOMEWHERE

I shouldn't be texting Rox behind Malcolm's back. It feels sneaky and wrong and the type of thing Gee would tell me to "leave off" doing if he was talking. I get up and start bouncing on my toes. I need to do something or go somewhere.

"Hey, Gee," I say. "You want to get out of the house for a while? Go out to your chair in the backyard?"

Gee doesn't answer me, but he grips the arms of his chair, and suddenly it's as if electricity filled the room.

"Come on," I say.

I help him up even though he doesn't seem to need it.

Except for not talking, it's hard to tell there's anything wrong with Gee. Mama says he was lucky because sometimes people who have strokes can't even come home for a while. They have to go stay somewhere trying to get stronger and move how they used to. Gee would've hated that.

Gee starts toward the front door, and I basically have no choice except to follow him. "Um, are you sure you want to go out front, Gee?"

Gee keeps moving resolutely to the door until all I can do is reach for the heavy knob and turn it.

Outside, a slight breeze tickles the leaves of the tall birch trees, and the sun finds the part in my hair, warming up that little road of scalp. The green, green grass, which Mama says is embarrassing because it means we're watering more than we should, glistens.

"It's nice out here, isn't it, Gee?" I ask. Maybe Gee's right. Maybe the best thing to do when you have a problem is to go outside.

Gee hustles down the walkway, me steady gripping his arm. I don't know what I'll do if he keeps going when he gets all the way to the sidewalk. I didn't think this idea through. And just like I was afraid of, when we get to the sidewalk, Gee doesn't even pause, and I have no choice but to go along with him. I throw a frightened look over my shoulder. This was a bad idea.

At the house next door, Gee turns up the walkway. This is Mrs. Woodley's house. She is nice and very old. Most of the people on our street are old.

When we get to Mrs. Woodley's front door, Gee pats his pockets and looks around. And then he gets an expression of panic on his face, and seeing him look like a scared little boy hurts my heart. It feels like it's getting squeezed. I need to get him back home.

I start pulling at his arm. "Come on, Gee," I say. "Come on, let's go back."

I'm sweating, and Gee is clearly looking for something, and at first, I worry that he's looking for that little gun, but when he opens Mrs. Woodley's shiny white mailbox, I know what he must be looking for. Not the gun, but mail. Like when he worked for the post office. Mama said all the little strokes made Gee's brain sort of fuzzy, and probably the big one did more damage. I think he's forgotten he isn't a mail carrier anymore. That gives me an idea of how to get him back inside. "You left your mail sack at the last house," I say. I don't know why I didn't say *our* house, except maybe if Gee is imagining he's delivering mail, it will make more sense in his head if this is all part of his route. "Come on, let's go back and get it."

That brings a smile to Gee's face, and it feels good knowing I put it there.

Back at our house, before I can open the door, it swings open, and Malcolm steps outside.

"Oh, there you are," he says. He has both crutches under one arm and his car keys in his other hand.

"Going somewhere?" I ask him.

"I was fixin' to . . . um, get something to eat," Malcolm says, sounding like he's lying. I wonder if he got a call from Rox. I hope so, so I don't say anything about all the food we have in the fridge. "You got this?" he asks me.

By *this*, he means Gee. "Yeah, sure," I say.

"I'll only be gone for a few. Just let Gee watch television. He likes that. Let's get him back inside."

I don't admit it to him, but I'm happy to have Malcolm's help with Gee. Once we're back inside I can relax.

As soon as we're through the door, Malcolm says, "Don't give Jenae a hard time, Gee," and leaves.

After the door closes, Gee looks at me expectantly.

"Let's get you back in your chair and—"

Gee makes a gurgling sound and grabs my arm. He gives it a hard squeeze.

I stare at him, and he stares right back, and it's like we're in one of those movies of his, doing a standoff. And I know who's going to win. Shoot.

I had thought Gee would forget about the mail once we were back inside, but obviously not. "Ooookay," I say. Taking Gee back outside isn't a great idea, but I don't see what choice I have.

I put both hands on his arms. "Wait right here." I dash over to the china cabinet. There's a built-in desk that looks just like another drawer until you pull it out, and then you can fold down the front of the drawer and that makes a flat surface to write on. And inside there are small cubbies for stationery and bills and stuff.

I grab a bunch of greeting cards charities send that Mama saves even though she never uses them. (*What if someone turns them over and sees I'm sending them a card I got for free?*) She says she keeps them *just in case*, and right now I'm glad she does. I put a bunch of cards in envelopes and look over my shoulder at Gee. He's just standing there, watching me and waiting.

I'm not really sure whether he'd notice the envelopes are blank, so I hurriedly write names like *Neighbor* and *Occupant* and then our street and city and zip code, just in case Gee is too smart to deliver mail to the wrong person. I throw a look over at him after each card. He hasn't moved. I make the last envelope out to Mrs. Woodley, just in case Gee wants to go next door again.

The envelopes look legit, except for not having stamps on them.

Mama would probably kill me if I wasted stamps on fake mail, but I'm not sure if Gee will deliver them if there's no postage. Then I remember my sticker collection that I put in one of the small drawers. The stickers look close enough to stamps, so I start putting them on. I look at Gee again, and now he's swaying a little. "Hold on, Gee!" I call out.

After the last sticker is attached, I yank a bag out of one of the drawers and shove the envelopes inside. Then I rush back to Gee. He grins at me in a way that makes me think he knows we're about to get up to something. Or maybe he knows he's getting the heck out of Dodge.

"Okay, look, we've got mail to deliver," I say, opening the bag and showing him the envelopes and saying a silent prayer he doesn't look too close. I turn him around, and we go back outside, and I'm thinking that either I'm a genius or really dumb.

Gee and I walk down the street, delivering our mail. When

we get to Tía Rosalie's house, just as Gee is about to slide one of our cards into the mailbox, Tía Rosalie surprises us by opening her door.

"Jenae! Grady!" she says, as if she's been waiting for us all day. "It's so nice seeing you." She's smiling, but her eyes go back and forth between me and Gee, questioning.

"Buenas tardes," I say. Tía Rosalie taught me how to say simple stuff in Spanish, and she always is happy when I show her I remember. She smiles and gives me a little nod. "We're just out delivering some mail," I explain. I hope she doesn't make a big deal about the mail not being real.

"Gracias," she says, taking the envelope from Gee's hand. "I always love getting cards." She slides out the card. "Oh, how did you know?" She turns the card around so I can see it was one of the *Congratulations!* ones. "I just heard my daughter got a promotion. I'm so happy for her. And now I have something to brag about when Mathilde gets going about her kids."

I grin at her for playing along with us. Gee and Tía Rosalie used to share seeds and cuttings from their yards. I'm not sure if they still do, but her eyes are so warm and friendly when she looks at him. If Gee were talking, the two of them would start chatting away in Spanish. He learned Spanish in school and never forgot it. He says it's easy in Los Angeles because lots of people speak Spanish here. Maybe one day I'll learn more than a couple of words.

"I heard you were in the hospital," Tía Rosalie tells Gee.

"Hard to believe. You look fine to me. Better than fine, no? Muy bien. How are you feeling?"

One side of Gee's mouth smiles at her.

"He's fine, Tía Rosalie," I answer for him.

She nods at that. "My cousin Reuben? Three *months* he stayed at a rehabilitation center after his stroke. Couldn't move much at all at first. But look at you—you'll be back running the streets in no time," she tells Gee. "Maybe you can come up to the school with me next time I go, eh?" Then she invites us in for hot cocoa, and before I can tell her, *No, thank you*, Gee takes a step forward.

I've never been inside Tía Rosalie's house before, but it's almost exactly like our house. The walls are painted a different color, but I'm sure behind the door in her dining room is the kitchen, and right off the kitchen there is most likely a breakfast nook and a big service porch.

Even though I've known Tía Rosalie all my life, it feels strange to be inside her house. But Gee follows her to the kitchen like it's the most normal thing, so I follow right behind him.

I expect Tía Rosalie to whip out packs of instant hot cocoa, but instead she pours milk into a pot on the stove and turns on the flame. Then she breaks chunks of hard chocolate from a package and drops the chunks into the milk. She plops some cinnamon sticks in too. Gee settles comfortably in a chair at her kitchen table like he's been there a hundred times.

"Have you ever had Mexican hot chocolate before?" Tía

Rosalie asks over her shoulder, and I shake my head. "Ah, then you're in for a treat."

She turns down the flame under the pot and keeps stirring.

"Tía Rosalie, *why* are people protesting at our school?" I ask. "I mean I know it's about the name, but is that really going to change people's minds?"

"My cousin Hector said more people need to show up. Make sure people know how we feel."

"Will it . . . um, make a difference, though?" I don't see how people standing in front of the school is going to make the school board decide on a name.

Tía Rosalie leans over the pot and fans the steam toward her face. "Ah, almost ready," she says. She looks over her shoulder at me. "To tell you the truth, I don't know if it will. But it felt good to be out there. Do you know I met a woman today from Guatemala?"

"She traveled all the way from Guatemala?" I ask.

Tia Rosalie's laughter fills the kitchen. "No! Her people, you know, are from Guatemala. She lives in Northridge but drove all the way here to support the school name change. It feels nice, all of us coming together. We all know this name change is important and that staying silent won't help. The board meeting is coming soon. And the people on the board get elected. They must do what the people want."

"But it seems like a lot of people are against changing the name."

She looks at Gee. "We know all about this problem, eh,

Grady?" she asks, and I want to tell her that he's not talking, but she must know, because she doesn't wait for an answer. "Some people think only their history is worthy of honor."

"But why?" I ask.

"This is a good question, but I don't have an answer for you. Why do people fight so hard to keep calling sports teams by hurtful names? As if tradition is more important than what's right?" She goes back to stirring.

"Some people feel like something is being taken from them, but seems to me that it is giving people something important. To know you've stood for what's right and honored someone truly important. What a gift. It's time for change, right, Grady?" She glances over at Gee. He doesn't answer, but that doesn't stop her for a second. "Right!" she says, and smiles at him just as if he agreed with her. "It may take many strong voices at the school board meeting to make sure they do the right thing."

I think about the people who have been outside of school with fliers and posters and how they'll probably be at the school board meeting too. "Do you think there's more people who want it changed than don't want it?"

"There *must* be," Tía Rosalie says, and I can't tell if she is just hoping so or if she knows so. She turns off the flame and pours out three steaming cups of cocoa. When she hands me my cup, the smell is so fantastic, at first I just sit there inhaling big whiffs. Gee starts drinking his right away. I take my first sip, and it's delicious. Thick chocolate and a tiny hint of cinnamon.

"Mmm," I say, and lick my lips. Gee takes a big loud slurp and that cracks Tía Rosalie up.

"It's delicious, right?" Tía Rosalie asks, and then nods as if she's answering herself. "I love this country, but Mexico will always have the best hot cocoa, and always a piece of my heart. Yes, there's a lot about my culture to celebrate."

Even though it's not my culture she's talking about, I feel like we're on the same side. And it makes me realize our school's name isn't about being against anything, it's all about being *for* something. If I was going to give a speech, I would make sure that point came across loud and clear. I'm still glad I won't be giving one, though. Just thinking about it makes my mouth go sour, and the cocoa doesn't taste so good anymore.

I thank Tía Rosalie and get Gee up and out.

As we walk back down the walkway, I can tell Gee has a little extra pep in his step. I need to get him back home, but it seems like being outside and doing his old routine might be helping him.

All while we head back down the street, I pepper Gee with questions, trying to get him to talk. What Mama told me about Gee sounds like he's just choosing to stay quiet, so I figure if I can ask him something interesting enough, he won't be able to help but answer. And he seems like he's in a good mood, so maybe that'll make him want to talk.

But things that usually get him going, like Lakers basketball, gardening, favorite drives, the cost of stuff now versus when he was my age, aren't getting a peep out of him. Birds dart around from tree to tree and they are doing lots of talking, but Gee stays quiet.

"Do you think Sylvia ever got mad at her parents for making her go to that school?"

He doesn't answer.

"I don't know if I would've been mad, but I sure would've been scared. What if someone was mean? What if they threw things at me? Would you have been scared?"

Gee doesn't answer.

"Were you scared when you delivered mail? Is that why you had the gun?"

The corner of Gee's mouth edges up, but I'm not sure if he's smiling or trying to say something.

I bet Sylvia would've made herself invisible if she could. "If I knew people might shout mean things at me, I think I'd be too afraid to leave the house."

Gee stops us in the middle of the sidewalk and faces me. He has a storm brewing in his eyes, and his mouth is scrunched into a frown.

Gee thinks being afraid is about the worst thing you can be. When I was six and didn't want to get into Aunt Jackie and Uncle Phil's pool, he made a huge deal about it and said I better get in before he tossed me in. I wasn't sure if he was serious, but I knew I better jump into that pool. And I didn't tell him that day, but the moment my toes left the wet concrete, that one second I had in the air before my belly slapped the water, I felt a little like a superhero.

He doesn't say anything, but his head shakes a little. Maybe it's just him trembling, but it seems like he's telling me no.

I can't imagine what he would say about me not being able to give my part of the speech. If he could, he'd probably throw me in front of my class and demand I do it. I get nauseous at the thought. "Okay, Gee, we got our mail all delivered. Let's take a break, okay?" I ask.

Although Gee doesn't answer, he must agree, because he lets me lead him back home.

Gee grasps the handrail to help him get up the front steps. Luckily, there's only five of them, and they are nice and wide.

"I'll get us something cool to drink," I tell Gee as we walk through the front door. Malcolm's not back, and that makes me smile; I'm sure after my text, Rox reached out and now he's visiting her! She'll make him happy.

But by the time I get back from the kitchen with two glasses of water, Gee's already snoring away. Mail delivery is exhausting. I'm feeling worn-out too. I didn't realize worry is hard work. It's like climbing a mountain. But I start on my homework instead of dozing off like I want to.

A phrase from Malcolm's basketball playing pops into my head: *No harm, no foul.* I don't know if I'd be in trouble for taking Gee out like I did, but he's fine, and I'm fine, so no foul.

When Malcolm gets back, he doesn't have any food with him, and he was gone for a long time. Long enough to maybe see an ex-girlfriend.

"Sorry," he says. "I got caught up, but no problems?" he asks me.

I shake my head and start picking at little tufts of fabric on the couch pillows. "Probably nice to get a break, huh?" I feel nervous, like he can see through me. If he saw Rox, did she tell him anything about our texting each other?

"It was all right," he says, and I see the smallest hint of a smile. It's not much, but it's progress. Now that Malcolm's moving in the right direction, it's time to take care of plan number two. The bad plan. The phrase comes into my head again. *No harm, no foul.* This plan is a foul for sure. I'll be harming Aubrey by not showing up. And if Mama finds out, she'll be so disappointed and angry. Plus she's sure to punish me, and that's harm to me. But facing a whole room full of people who are staring at me, and judging me and seeing how I don't know anything and can't get my mouth to cooperate? Standing in a puddle of sweat so big it will probably drown me? And my sweat stinking up the whole place? That's harm too. I can't give the speech. My dad *has* to get me out of it.

Before I can change my mind, I quickly type a message to my dad letting him know I need a favor.

I've set the groundwork, and it makes me feel frozen inside.

41
PILE OF LIES

It's time to go to bed and I still haven't heard back from my dad. I keep checking and checking, but I only get messages from Aubrey. Some facts about Sylvia Mendez. A message saying how hard it must've been for her and how maybe she didn't have any friends when she was going to school. Each message makes me feel worse, and I respond with only one-word answers. He'll be so upset when I'm not there on Wednesday.

I click on the message I sent my dad. Maybe he hasn't answered because he thinks I might be asking for too big a favor, so I type:

I just need you to pick me up from school early next Wednesday.

I stare at the message for a full minute, sucking my bottom lip. My lungs don't seem to be working right, or have shrunk down to grape size. I still don't see any other choice. I press send.

Before I get into bed, I check my phone one more time, and I still don't have a message from my dad, but I have another from Aubrey.

I'm glad we're friends.

I stare at the word *friends* for a long, long time. I went from having no friends to having one. And it's scary to admit, but having a friend, even one as over-the-top as Aubrey, feels better than having no one.

I feel like an awful person. I should text my dad back and tell him never mind. But then what?

I text Aubrey back:

Me too.

And get an immediate smiley face back.

I stare at my ceiling for a long time before finally falling asleep.

When I wake up in the morning, I see my dad texted me in the middle of the night. He's probably in another time zone, because he couldn't think I would be awake at two o'clock in the morning.

As long as it's okay with your mother.

I text back that Mama said it was fine, she's just too busy at work to do it herself, and try not to think about how many lies are piling up and how lying is a really terrible thing to do.

Just pick me up from school at 10.

I could have him pick me up right after lunch, but I doubt I could sit next to Aubrey all through lunch pretending I'm going to be around for fifth period. I'll see him in history, and then that will be it.

And if my dad picks me up and brings me home before six,

Mama won't ever even know I missed a day of school. I probably should be worrying less about getting busted and more about how bad it is what I'm doing. Even though I don't understand why Aubrey cares about dumb debate club, he does. A *lot*. And I'm lying to Mama and my dad too. All of it is so wrong.

Mama drops me off at the corner instead of pulling into the drop-off zone the next day. She says she doesn't want to be hassled by the crowd that seems like it's getting bigger each day. My feet feel heavy as I walk to the front of the school. Tía Rosalie isn't there today, which is a little disappointing. I could use her smiling face. She has a way of making me feel better.

I'm not looking forward to seeing Aubrey. Now that I've actually asked my dad to get me out of school, I feel like there's this huge big deal between us. I'm dreading what's going to happen. I know if I tried to explain again about not being able to give a speech, Aubrey would argue and say it's just nerves. He might even say it was quack. Or that *I* was quack.

At lunch, Aubrey asks me if I've decided what side I want to take for our speech. Since I know I won't be doing it at all, it doesn't matter, and I figure the fair thing to do, the *nice* thing to do, would be for Aubrey to get to pick the side he wants.

"What side do *you* want?" I ask over my crunchy gherkins. I love all sorts of pickles, but the tiny ones are my favorite. They're so cute.

"Well, the side I'm *on* is changing the name. But it's harder to represent the side you don't you really believe in, and I know you don't like giving speeches, so I should probably take the tougher side. Click, right?"

"Right," I say, not wanting to argue. "I guess it's . . . click." I feel a little silly using that word.

He raises his water bottle and taps it against mine like we're doing cheers.

Then he says, "It's funny how you don't like giving speeches and I love doing them! Especially when it's going to be a debate! In Chicago, I even went to a debate *camp*. It was so sway, and I learned a bunch. I'm like a secret weapon! No one knows how good I am at this. You got the best partner!"

I don't see what's funny about it. It's just a clear sign that we're not meant to be friends.

But I'm sure he is right about me getting the best partner. Unfortunately, he got the worst.

42

COWBOYS

After school, our principal, Mr. Martinez, is telling people they can't stand in front of the school since they are getting in the way of students trying to leave. He and some of the teachers have them go stand on the other side of the street.

One group is dressed in cowboy boots and hats and they have signs showing a smiling John Wayne. A woman with a long ponytail is sticking fliers through windows into the cars in the pickup lane, but Mr. Martinez doesn't make her stop.

I'm surprised to see blazing-red hair right in the middle of the cowboy group. He sees me too and waves me over like his arm is a windmill. I take a step back. I don't want to go over there. But then he hollers, "Jenae! Jenae!" and his windmill arm is now caught in a storm, whipping around frantically like I might not see him.

In order to make him stop making a spectacle of both of us, I force myself to cross the street and join him.

"I'm collecting info for our speech!" he says. "They want the school to stay John Wayne Junior High."

Since I know Aubrey isn't actually for our school staying John Wayne, I'm surprised he sounds so excited. I feel embarrassed, especially since some people holding Sylvia Mendez pictures and SAY YES TO CHANGE! signs are looking over like we're against them.

Aubrey points to a man standing close by. "He's the head of the committee!" The man has friendly blue eyes, and he doesn't seem to mind when Aubrey asks him why he doesn't want the name to change.

"Too many people want to change the past," he says. "History is important. This school was John Wayne Junior High when I went here. There's no good reason to change it."

"But do you know about Sylvia Mendez?" Aubrey asks. "About people not wanting her to go to their school just because she wasn't white?"

I can't believe Aubrey asked that, even if it's true. Honestly, I can't believe Aubrey is talking to this man at all. My mouth is getting tight, and I'm not even the one saying anything.

I can tell Aubrey's question bothered cowboy-boot man, but his eyes haven't gone mean. "Lookit," he says. "What happened back then? Trash. Complete trash. But that was a long time ago. And it didn't even happen at this school."

The woman with the fliers moves nearer to us. "We're right by Hollywood," she says. "John Wayne was a *Hollywood* star." She is talking to us like we're dumb and don't know who John Wayne was.

"What about John Wayne making racist comments when

he was alive?" Aubrey asks, not sounding mad but just curious.

The man sighs, and the woman gets an angry look, and I just want to leave.

"It was a different time," the man says. "And when you think about what he said, he wasn't saying anything different from what a whole lot of people were thinking at the time."

One thing about Astrid Dane is, no matter what time she's living in, when something's wrong, it's still wrong.

"Besides," the woman says, "you can't believe everything you read, kids. And they sure can honor anyone they like, as long as they leave this school alone." She nods, like *case closed*, and moves back to the line of cars idling in the pickup line so she can go back to shoving fliers through people's windows.

I don't like the way she said *they*.

"Come on," I tell Aubrey. "Let's go."

"The school board isn't going to change the name," the man calls after us. "Too many people are against it. They'll definitely see that at the board meeting."

Oh, yeah? I think. It's right on the tip of my tongue to say, but I don't let the words out. I didn't think I cared that much what our school was called, but now I sure hope that man is wrong. I really want the school's name to be changed to Sylvia Mendez, and I'm glad Aubrey thinks so too.

43

NOT EXACTLY LYING

"Hey, do you have to go straight home?" Aubrey asks.

I actually don't know. This question has never come up before, since I never had any place to go after school except home.

"Why?" I ask, stalling.

"Do you want to go to my mom's restaurant?"

"S-s-sure," I stutter. "What's she like?"

Aubrey frowns. "She worries too much," he says, and it's the first time I've heard him sound sort of angry, but he rubs a hand over his face, and it's as if he wiped the bad feeling away, because when he puts his hand down, he's smiling again. "She *used* to, anyway. Now she's pretty sway, I guess."

"Let me just text Malcolm to let him know." My hands tremble a little as I take out my phone. I text Malcolm, and Aubrey watches me, and I shove my phone into my bag trying to pretend that texting my brother to tell him I'm hanging out with a friend after school is the most normal thing ever. My mouth is dry, so I try to swallow a few times.

"Come on," Aubrey says, and I follow him going the opposite direction than I normally go.

It feels okay. Strange, but okay.

The restaurant where Aubrey's mom works isn't that far from school, and it is probably the cutest place I've ever seen. It's called Nook, and stepping inside is like walking into a fairy tale. There are little tables and frilly curtains and tiny white lights running across the ceiling and down the walls. There are paintings of large brown women holding fruit, and baskets of fresh vegetables and piles of bread lining a counter. It feels cozy and special at the same time, and it smells like heaven.

A short smiling woman with blondish hair in a big sloppy bun comes out of the kitchen and greets Aubrey with a hug and big smacking kiss on the check. "My boy!" she says, as if seeing Aubrey is the best thing that has ever happened to her.

I'm not surprised at all that Aubrey's mom is white. As fair as he is, I figured he was mixed. I also figured a Black mom wouldn't let her kid dye their hair like that. At least not any Black mom I've met.

"Ma, quit it," Aubrey says, squirreling out of her grip. "I have company!"

His mom's eyes light on me, and she dusts off her flour-covered hands on her bright red apron, leaving white handprints on her hips. She looks older than Mama, and maybe older than any of the moms I'm used to seeing picking up kids from school. It's funny to me that she has a bright blue streak in her hair, and a few tattoos on her arms, because it doesn't seem like something someone her age would do.

She thrusts her right hand out to shake mine. I can see one of her tattoos is swirly lettering that spells out *Tasty*. "Hi! Hi! I'm Ellen Banks, Aubrey's mother, obviously. So nice to meet you!"

I see where Aubrey gets his need to talk in exclamation marks. I wonder if the two of them are just exhausted at the end of the day. That's a whole lot of energy to put into talking.

"Hi," I say shyly, extending my hand to meet hers. "I'm Jenae." We shake, and I feel the soft silt of flour.

"Oh, Jenaaay," she says, and gives Aubrey a nod. "I've heard so much about you."

Aubrey goes so red, his face almost matches his hair. "Ma!"

"Oh, sorry, I'm being a little extra, aren't I?" Mrs. Banks asks me, and then winks. "Can I get you two something to eat?"

"Sure!" Aubrey says.

Mrs. Banks looks at her watch. "We don't open for dinner until five, so I have just enough time to make you something quick before I have to finish my prep."

Aubrey goes over to a small table in the corner and beckons me to follow him, but his mom rests a hand on my shoulder, keeping me next to her.

A voice shouts from the kitchen, "Ellen, you want these tarts to go in the oven?"

"Hold on, I'll do it," Mrs. Banks hollers back. Then she bends close to me. "I'm so glad Aubrey has made a friend here," she says. "It's so hard when you've been homeschooled to know how to fit in. I hope you're being kind to him."

Homeschooled?

She gives my shoulder a squeeze, leaving a faint white hand-print, and then rushes back into the kitchen.

I slowly make my way to the table. I think of things Aubrey said about Chicago and friends. I don't think he ever talked about school, but it still feels like he lied to me somehow. I sit across from him, wondering what I should say.

"My mom makes these apple tarts that are so good, but those won't be ready for a while. Did she say she'd make calamari?" He smacks his lips. "Best snack ever! Or maybe the best is her spicy wings!"

I decide to test him. "Your friends back in Chicago must've loved how good a cook your mom is."

"Click! You know it. She'd cook for us all the time!"

I can't tell if Aubrey is lying, but he's not meeting my eyes, and that's a bad sign.

"Did they, um, come over a lot? Or did she, like, work in a restaurant there that you guys would go to?" I'm not sure why I feel so nervous when I'm not doing anything wrong. Asking Aubrey about his friends should be totally fine . . . if he really had them.

Aubrey looks up at me and then looks away. He tries to laugh, but it doesn't sound right. "She didn't work at a restaurant there, remember? She did taxes. She just practiced her cooking at home."

Right away I notice how he avoided answering my question straight on. Another bad sign. "What was the name of your school in Chicago?" I ask. "Was it named after anybody?"

Aubrey doesn't say anything for a minute, and then, looking hugely embarrassed, he asks, "She told you, huh?"

I don't even know what to say. He was just tricking me all this time? I get up fast, and my chair almost crashes over. "I cannot *believe* you," I hiss at him. I start to walk away, ready to get as far from Aubrey as I can, but he gets up and grabs my arm.

"Let me go!" I tell him angrily.

"Okay! Okay!" he says, letting go of my arm and raising both of his hands.

And then we just stand there facing each other.

"You lied to me," I finally say.

"Not really," Aubrey says, lowering his arms. "At least, it wasn't exactly lying. It's just that, I don't— I didn't— I . . ." I expect him to start twisting his little unicorn horn, but he doesn't. His arms stay down at his sides, and his hands are still. He's watching me, and his usual smile is so deeply buried under sadness, or maybe regret, that it's hard to believe it has ever lived on his face. "No one actually . . ."

He is having trouble finishing a sentence, and I want to shake him.

"I don't understand what you mean," I say, even though an idea is starting to creep up the back of my neck. "Why would you trick me like that?"

"I really didn't mean to! But you don't know what it's like being the weird kid."

"Are you *serious* right now? *I* don't know what it's like? Me? Do you pay attention to me at all? Who I actually am, not who you *want* me to be?" I don't give him a chance to answer. "Obviously not! You don't know one thing about me!" I turn away from him then, and my plan is to walk out of the restaurant and stomp off down the street and leave him all by his dumb self, but I can't. I feel frozen like a huge slab of ice, and I just stand with my back to him, trying to breathe and staring at a painting of a woman dancing on a piece of honeydew melon. I think of all the stuff he told me.

"You talked about your friends. And what you guys do. And what you guys *say*!" What a dummy I was, thinking all those made-up words were real. He must've laughed at me every day. The woman on the melon has her mouth open in laughter, and it feels like she's laughing at me too.

"Jenae," Aubrey says softly. "I'm sorry. I just wanted to be sway. I—I mean cool." His voice is rough and shaky. "Just for once," he adds softly.

It almost makes me laugh. Because the truth is, everything Aubrey did was so spectacularly *un*cool.

"I was sick a lot," he says. "With the leukemia and everything, and so that's why I was homeschooled."

That makes me turn back around. "But kids who are homeschooled still do stuff and have activi—"

"It wasn't like that for me. My mom was nervous about me catching somebody's cold or whatever. It could've been dangerous to get sick like that while I was having cancer treatments." Aubrey looks over his shoulder nervously and then takes a step closer to me and lowers his voice. "But she took it too far. She didn't let me go to anyone's house, or go to group activities, or let anyone come over. She . . . she was scared."

Even though it sounds like Aubrey is standing up for his mom, he sounds angry at her.

"You could've told me all that," I say.

"Everyone thinks it's weird, that *I'm* weird, if I say I didn't go to regular school. And that I didn't have . . ."

He doesn't finish his sentence, but I can guess he was going to say that he didn't have friends. And now I feel bad for making him have to admit it. My frozen edges begin to thaw.

"I wouldn't have thought that," I say softly. I wonder if he felt as if he were invisible. "I would've thought it was interesting."

"Maybe you haven't noticed this, but you're not like other people."

I don't know if I should be insulted or complimented.

"Will you . . . can we sit back down?" Aubrey asks.

I don't want to stomp off anymore. I actually don't know how I feel. Maybe more like I'm a slushy instead of frozen hard. And when Aubrey turns and goes back to the table, I go ahead and follow him.

Mrs. Banks returns with two big glasses of what looks like

both lemonade and orange juice. It's yellow at the bottom half, and the top is orange, slowly sinking into the yellow. It looks delicious. "Sunsets for two!" she says. "Have you decided what you want to eat?"

I want to taste the drink, but I'm not sure if you're supposed to stir it up first or not.

Aubrey glances at me and then asks his mom to bring us something delicious.

"You got it, kids!" she says, and bustles back to the kitchen.

"I'm sorry I didn't tell you," Aubrey says, his voice low.

"Still friends?" he asks, and smiles hopefully at me.

The drink in front of me is begging for me to take a sip out of it. That's how delicious it looks. Two different flavors, both yummy, and ready to be blended together and made even better. "Yeah," I say, the word catching a bit in my throat. In my head I add, *At least until Wednesday.*

His smile grows, and it's basically impossible not to smile back at that mile-wide grin of his, and the last bit of ice surrounding me defrosts.

I grin back at him.

Aubrey's smile gets so big I am positive it's just going to gobble his whole face, and then he starts cracking up, which makes me laugh. And then we're both laughing super hard and I don't care if he didn't tell me he was homeschooled and that he just makes up random words, and I stir up my sunset drink and take a huge satisfying slurp.

Mrs. Banks comes back with a steaming plate. "Try this,"

she says, setting it down in front of us. "Something new I'm trying. Mini grilled cheese sandwiches."

There's a collection of small sandwiches, all with cheese oozing from the sides. Orange cheese, white cheese, cheese with little black specks that taste like pepper. Each one I try is delicious. Salty and crunchy and buttery, and one is a tiny bit sweet.

Mrs. Banks stands there watching us eat, her hands pressed together and her forehead all creased with worry, waiting for the verdict.

"Oh, wow," I say, my mouth still full of a sandwich. I quickly swallow. "That's maybe the best thing I've ever tasted. What type of cheese is in this one?" I point to the one with white cheese and a bit of jam that's brown and maybe fig.

Mrs. Banks looks over both shoulders before leaning toward me and whispering, "Manchego, and that's *date* jam." She looks so pleased with herself, and her smile is about as big as Aubrey's.

"It's so good," I say, and I don't even like dates.

"You really like them?" she asks in a small squeal, and her face brightens up with a huge smile. She claps. "Yay!"

Aubrey rolls his eyes. "I told you."

"Do you think I should serve them with tomato soup?" Mrs. Banks asks me.

I pop another small sandwich into my mouth and then I smile at her. "Definitely."

A smiling woman comes from the kitchen. She has big brown happy eyes, and her hair is in really long braids. *White* braids. They look really cool against her dark skin, but as young as her face looks, it's hard to believe her hair could've gone gray, so maybe she had it dyed white. "How many people are you going to test those sandwiches on before you believe us?" she asks Mrs. Banks.

"I know. I know," Mrs. Banks says, blushing. "But this is your place, Dom. I don't want to mess with it."

Dom puts her hands on her narrow hips and gives Mrs. Banks one of those looks. Mama calls it the *Girl, please* look. "You think I'd let you mess this place up?"

It's funny how Mrs. Banks looks too old for tattoos, and Dom looks too young for white hair.

Mrs. Banks laughs. "Okay, kiddos, we have lots of prep left to do before the dinner crowd. So finish up and skedaddle. And, Aubrey," she adds sternly. "You make sure you answer me when I text you."

Aubrey rolls his eyes. "If you don't text me every five seconds I will."

I hold my breath, waiting for Mrs. Banks to go off on Aubrey like Mama would with me if I talked back like that, but she just gives one of his curls a little pull and then laughs.

"Go on, you two!" she says.

When we step back into the sunshine, it's a shock. There are so many people walking down the sidewalk; horns are honking, and the big security gates rattle and boom.

We start walking back the way we came. I'm not sure if Aubrey plans on walking with me all the way to my house. I haven't invited him over, but it's not as if that would stop him.

"So that's my mom," Aubrey says. "Sorry she's so . . . extra."

"Like you," I can't resist saying, and Aubrey fake frowns like I've hurt his feelings. "What's your dad like?" I ask.

Aubrey stops in the middle of the sidewalk, and his frown doesn't look fake anymore. "He, uh . . ."

"That's okay," I say hurriedly. "You don't have to say." I know I've asked a bad question. I don't know why it's bad, but I know I shouldn't have asked.

Aubrey shakes his head. "No, it's okay. It's just that . . ." He takes a big breath. "He died. When I was really little. He had cancer too."

"I'm sorry," I whisper.

"Thanks," Aubrey says. "But there's nothing for you to be sorry for."

"I know," I say. *But isn't that what you're supposed to say? I wonder.*

"Hey, I bet I can beat you to the end of the block!" Aubrey says, and crouches down into a ready position.

"Bet you can't!" I yell, and take off running, and when Aubrey blazes past me, I don't even mind.

44

FRIENDSHIP CALENDAR

When I get home, Gee's eyes open wide, and then he starts pressing his hands into the armrests of his big chair, pushing himself up.

"Dang, Jenae, I didn't know you were going to be so long!" Malcolm complains. "Gee's been all jumpy waiting for you."

"Waiting for me? Why?"

"Don't ask me," Malcolm says. "But ever since the mail came, he's been up and out of his chair and looking out the window for you." He nods his head at the small stack of mail on the table by the door.

I look at the mail, and then back at Gee, who is now standing up. He looks excited, and I realize he's been waiting to deliver more mail. "Oh," I say. I don't think delivering mail with Gee is a bad thing to do, but Malcolm might think it's dumb, or that it's too much walking for Gee. I twist my hands together, unsure.

Malcolm stands up and stretches big. His hands reach high above his head, and I marvel for a second at how tall my brother is and how long his arms are. And how if you ignore the big brace, he looks like he is maybe the most in-shape person ever.

As if he heard my thoughts, he bends down and unstraps the brace. He bends his leg a few times, getting it loose, but then he grunts and straps the brace back on.

"Does it still hurt?" I force myself to ask.

Malcolm's eyes darken. "All the time," he says. "You set with Gee? I'm going to take a break upstairs. Only so many Westerns I can sit through." I nod, and he makes his way to the stairs, doing the hoppy-step thing he does when he's not using crutches.

I wish I had thought to bring some of the tiny grilled cheese sandwiches home with me. It wouldn't have helped his knee, but I bet enjoying those bites of buttery goodness sure would have made him feel better for a minute. When he gets all the way up the stairs, I do the next best thing. I pull out my phone and send Rox a text. About how I'm guessing she called him because he is smiling more and how physical therapy really helps Malcolm and he should go more. I don't even feel guilty this time. Rox seems happy to help Malcolm, so what's the harm?

"Okay, Gee," I say, putting my phone away. "Let's get some mail delivered." I toss my book bag on the couch and rush over to the desk and get some more envelopes ready. I don't make as many as I did yesterday. It's already sort of late, and I have homework.

By the time I have the stack ready, Gee is at the front door, his hand on the knob.

"Wait for me, Gee!" I call out.

I sure hope once we get outside, I'll be able to get him back in.

Mail delivery goes smoothly, and when we get back, Malcolm is downstairs, talking on the phone. But as soon as we walk in, he tells the person he has to go. He doesn't sound happy about it.

"I'll sit with Gee, Malcolm," I say, hoping he was talking to Rox and that she was taking his mind off things. Maybe even encouraging him to go to physical therapy. Whether he plays again or not, he needs to make sure his knee heals the way it's supposed to. "You can talk upstairs. It's sway."

A bit of relief peeks from Malcolm's eyes, and he nods at me, but then he asks, "Sway?"

I rock my hands back and forth like we're sailing, or gliding. Now that I know Aubrey's words are made up, it's almost more fun to use them. "Yep," I say. "Totally sway."

He rolls his eyes, but then says, "Thanks."

Once he's upstairs, a feeling of pride settles over me like a comfy blanket, and I start to hum as I get out my books to start homework, but then all of a sudden it's like someone ripped the blanket off and replaced it with an itchy coat. Having someone nudge him to get on with his life is what Malcolm needs, but if it's the right thing to do, why do I have to be so secretive about it? I'm smart enough to know that doing something behind someone's back isn't cool. That makes me think about what I'm doing to Aubrey. I'm pretending to him like I'm going to give the speech with him, when I know I'm not.

What kind of friend does that make me?

When one of the ghosts takes over Astrid Dane, it's like she's not herself anymore. Instead, for a while she becomes a witch, or a clown, or a farmer. She can't control it and she's not a huge fan of the feeling. I think I know what that must be like, because right now it's as if an out-of-control monster has taken over me and I can't stop it from doing what it wants.

In my room that night, I sit at my desk and make a small calendar. It's only this week and next week. Not even the whole month.

I have six days left to be friends with Aubrey. And that doesn't seem like a lot, but that's a lot more days of friendship than I've ever had before, so I should just enjoy them. Next Wednesday, when I don't show up, it will be over. But I still have six days. And some of those days are the weekend. Aubrey and I can go to the library and go to the park and try to climb around stuff like Astrid Dane does. We can go to the mall and follow people like spies. Maybe I can make him a vest too. I wonder if he likes movies. I like all different kinds of movies, except the very scary ones. Malcolm loves those. Probably because he doesn't think they are scary at all. He laughs through them and talks about how fake the blood is, or how he knew someone was about to jump out of the closet.

Maybe Aubrey and I can just climb up in the apple tree in the backyard and pick fruit for Gee. I tap my pen against my teeth, trying to figure out what other types of things friends do together.

I wish we could go on an incredible adventure. Find a ship heading out to sea and stow away. I shake my head at myself for being so ridiculous.

Astrid Dane tries really hard not to make friends. They'd get old and she wouldn't, and then they'd find out her secret.

I wonder what Aubrey would say if he found out my secret. That hurting Malcolm and Gee isn't the worst thing I've done. Breaking up Mama and my dad is worse than that. If I told him, he wouldn't believe me. But I know the truth.

Maybe Astrid Dane has the right idea. And maybe things would've been better if Aubrey had never moved here.

Friendship seems all sorts of messy and hard.

45

A PAIR

When I make my lunch in the morning, I make a little extra so I can share with Aubrey. I even text him and ask whether he likes Anjou pears or Bosc. He texts me back a bunch of question marks, but then texts *Anjou*, so I start cutting up some of that kind.

"You and these lunches!" Mama says. "You must get these fancy ways from your father's side."

Her mentioning my dad makes me almost cut myself with the knife. If Mama ever finds out about him getting me out of school, I'll be in so much trouble.

In the car, we hear a news report about the upcoming school board meeting and how it's going to be "contentious." With a huff, Mama changes the station. "As if we don't have real problems," she mutters. "All this fuss about a name change."

"You don't think it's important, Mama?"

Mama snaps her head so fast in my direction, I swear she forgot I was even in the car. "I'm not saying that," she says. "Lord knows we need to do a better job of honoring folks in our community." She shakes her head, and her dangling blue earrings swing back and forth. "But people fighting so hard against it?" She shakes her head again. "Why aren't they fighting for new textbooks? Or basic school supplies?"

I wish I knew the answers.

She drops me off, and I hurry into school to meet up with Aubrey.

In history he leans over and asks what was up with the pears.

"You'll see," I say with a grin.

"Jenae," Geoffrey says, "can I borrow a pencil?"

I'm so shocked that Geoffrey actually knows my name that my hand shakes a little when I reach to get him a pencil from my bag. "Here," I say, trying to sound natural.

At lunch, almost as soon as he sits down, Aubrey says, "Lunch is so short." He takes the baggie I hold out to him full of sliced pears. "Maybe we should try sitting over there?" He nods his head toward the lunch area, with all its noise and people. "Get to eating faster?" He stuffs some pear into his mouth.

In my head, I see my friendship calendar with so few days. He'll be sitting over there at lunch soon enough. I shake my head. "I like it here. It's quieter."

Aubrey nods like he gets it. Like he gets me. "Okay," he says. "It's sway."

I feel like a piece of pear is stuck in my throat. Even though Aubrey didn't tell me the total truth about his life in Chicago, he's been a good friend. I *have* to give the speech. That's all there is to it. It's just a speech. It won't kill me. I can do it.

46

LAST THING ANYONE NEEDS

We head to English, and before we have a chance to take our seats and settle down, Mr. Humphries tells us to follow him to the auditorium.

He seems way too excited, and I'm immediately suspicious.

Our school has a real auditorium, not just a multipurpose room.

Someone—maybe it was John Wayne—donated a whole bunch of money when our school was built so it could have an auditorium with soft seats and a stage with a row of black curtains and lights like they have in the movies.

As soon as we get there, Mr. Humphries says, "Line up, everyone." He claps his hands. "I'm going to have you walk up on the stage and just belt out a sentence or two. Try to make them *why* sentences. It's how we begin an argument. Maybe tell us . . . why you like weekends, or why your best friend likes you, or why you hate brussels sprouts." He cracks up like he told the best joke. I do not laugh. I feel like someone punched me right in the stomach. "I want clear enunciation, and I want you to test your projection. Deliver your words to the very back row."

I straight up hate Mr. Humphries right now. I was absolutely, awfully right to have suspected something was up.

Even though I don't say how I feel out loud, Aubrey still gives me a nudge. "It's not a speech," he says. "Just some sentences. They can be short. Just make 'em loud."

Aubrey doesn't understand anything!

The lights are on in the auditorium, so I can't even dissolve into a shadow and float out in a wisp of noise and hot air. I would get busted for sure. I would be seen. Why is Mr. Humphries making us do this?

"Come on," Aubrey says. "We need to get in line."

"*You* do," I say. I can feel the whirring in my ears, and my stomach rolling and flipping. I can't get up on a stage and have everyone stare at me.

People in line are joking around as if having to go up on that stage and say something is no big deal. Like they all secretly were hoping to have a chance to star in their own personal movie. I have never wanted to be a star. I do not want to get up there. No way.

The red exit signs are glowing, calling my name and telling me how easy it would be to just run away. I bend over and scratch my knee. I scratch so hard it feels like I'm ripping through my skin. I feel dizzy and like I might pass out or throw up or both.

I watch as my classmates walk one by one to the middle of

the stage, say something, and then walk off. Omar Chalhoub tells us he likes playing football because he loves smashing into people. But as the next students go, a steady whirring noise is getting louder and louder in my ears. By the time it's almost my turn, I can't hear a word, and I can barely see. My stinky sweat burns my nose. I am going to swallow my tongue. I am going to barf.

Aubrey goes onstage, and I see his mouth moving, but I can't concentrate on his words. Even so, I want him to talk and talk and talk so that we never get to my turn, but then he smiles down at me and walks off the stage.

The person behind me nudges me, signaling that it's my turn. I don't move. I *want* to. That's the thing. I want to be able to walk right up on that stage and project a quick sentence and then walk back off, like no big deal. If I could, I would give a sentence about why I like the weather. Like how good sunshine feels on my face. Or how rain makes the world smell new and seems like a promise.

Mr. Humphries's mouth is moving as he stares at me. Somewhere, Aubrey is watching me, and maybe finally realizing he made a huge mistake asking me to be his partner.

I get another nudge, and I force my legs to move. Burning-hot tears pile up in my eyes, and my lips are clenched together so tight my teeth are cutting into them. *Weather. Weather. Weather*, I chant to myself. I can do this. It's just a sentence.

I reach the center of the stage and can't open my mouth. If I do, squeaky ear-piercing sounds will come out. Not words, just bird chirps and grunts. I'm shaking so hard my knees knock together, and my nails dig so hard into my palms it hurts, but I keep doing it.

I try to melt into the floor, but it doesn't work. I don't know how to be invisible anymore.

People are staring at me. Everyone in the room. So much sweat oozes down my legs, my shoes are probably getting full.

Why can't I be brave like Astrid Dane?

I unclench my lips and let my mouth fall open. I concentrate and try to form a word. I think of clouds and rainbows and fog so dense you feel alone in the world. My mouth is just hanging open. "I . . . ," I say. It feels like hours pass. ". . . like sunny rain because . . . sparkle." I definitely do not project. I walk off the stage and join the people who've already gone.

Someone near me giggles.

Aubrey is grinning and trying to talk to Grant Childress about chicken nuggets, and although Grant seems to be ignoring him, Aubrey looks calm and confident, and it is clear that he and I are nothing alike.

I can't do the speech. And pretty quick Aubrey will realize I did him a big, huge favor, because the last thing anyone needs is to be friends with me.

47

TRUE GRIT

After school, the people outside make me anxious and annoyed. Don't they have better things to do? Maybe everyone should just leave the school alone. Aubrey runs up like a puppy dog, acting like he expects to come over, but I tell him I have to go straight home and that Mama told me I couldn't have company. I don't know why I'm lying except I know having Aubrey over is inviting a whole bunch of speech talk.

"Okay," he says, sounding disappointed. "See you later."

My walk home is hot and feels longer than normal. I stop at the store hoping to make myself feel better with some Red Vines, but when I check my bag, I don't have any money, and I have to put the package back. When I make the turn onto our street, Tía Rosalie is out watering, and she tells me good afternoon in Spanish, and I raise my hand in an almost wave but don't stop. I don't feel like being friendly.

When I get home, Gee is of course in his chair, and Malcolm is over in the corner on the computer. He has headphones on and is drumming his hand to a beat. Guess he's downloading some new music.

Surprisingly, Gee isn't watching a Western. There's some big robot thing smashing a town, so I'm pretty sure it's something Malcolm wanted to watch.

With a glance at my brother, I squat next to Gee and whisper, "Have you ever had to do something, Gee, even though it maybe would hurt someone's feelings? Like you didn't have a single, solitary choice except to do it?"

Gee stares at me, his eyes so wide I can't help but think he's trying to say something. I stare at the blue around his irises. It's summer-sky blue. Frost Popsicle blue. Faded-jeans blue. His eyes might be hypnotizing me.

He makes a noise like he's trying to say something. "What is it, Gee? Are you okay?" I peek over at Malcolm, but he's totally unaware of us. Maybe I should tell him something's wrong with Gee.

I look back at Gee, and he opens his mouth, but no words come out.

"What, Gee?" I push the notepad at him, but he doesn't even look at it. I'm pretty sure I know what Gee would say if he could. He'd say that there is always a choice. And I feel guilty that I'm a tiny bit happy that I don't have to hear him say it.

"I *can't*, Gee. I know you said I need to face things I'm afraid of, but I *can't*." I grip his hand tight, trying to convince him, but he only blinks and then turns his head to the television like he's done with me.

To apologize, I turn on a Western. It's a John Wayne one. He's wearing a patch over one of his eyes. The movie is called *True Grit*, and I've seen it before, because it's one of Gee's favorites. There's a girl in it who's kind of obnoxious but also really brave.

The girl in the movie is more like Astrid Dane than me. Maybe it's grit. It doesn't sound like anything you'd want. But I think of how Astrid doesn't seem to be afraid of anything. And how if she had a brother, she never would've stopped him from playing basketball just because she missed him.

When Mama comes through the front door that night, she looks like she's had a long, hard day. Malcolm has disappeared.

Gee is rattling the windows with his snores, and Mama runs a hand over his back before heading to the kitchen. I follow her through the swinging door.

"I'm sorry I didn't start anything for dinner," I say. "You want me to make the pasta with broccoli that you like?"

Mama shakes her head. "Let's just order pizza. We can all have the night off."

That doesn't seem like anything Mama would say, but I'm not about to argue. I love pizza.

Mama goes over to the drawer where we keep all the take-out menus and starts riffling through, looking for the good pizza place. "Can you believe I got a call at work today about your school's name? I don't know how some random parent got my number, but I sure did block them." She tsk-tsks and shakes her head.

"I think it should change," I say, and it's the first time I've said it out loud. "What do you think, Mama?"

"You know, if you'd asked me a week ago, I probably would've said I didn't care one way or the other, but . . ." Her voice fades away, and she looks off into the distance. "I want it to change, I do. But getting my dad back, that's what I really want."

Gee hasn't left, but I know what Mama means. Without him talking to us, it does seem like he's not totally there. Gee has always had so much to say about everything. "The neurologist and the speech pathologist both said there doesn't seem to be any physical reason for him not talking," Mama says.

"I miss being able to talk to him," I say.

Mama doesn't say anything for a moment. "You know, Jenae, I know it's hard on you, not having your dad come around much."

I'm so surprised, I take a step back.

"Oh, I know how it is," Mama says. "Your dad just . . ."

I hold my breath, anxious to hear anything that might explain why I don't see him. Why he doesn't seem to be bothered very much about whether *he* sees *me*. Maybe he can feel a slight echo of me pushing him away all those years ago.

"Just what?" I ask when it doesn't seem as if Mama is going to finish her sentence.

She shakes her head. "Honestly, I wish I knew. But at least you've had your grandfather."

"I *have* my grandfather," I correct her.

She smiles at me. "That's right. That's what I meant. And you have *me*." Then she can't resist adding, "Shoot, that's a lot better than that man. Now let's get this pizza ordered." Mama finds the number of the pizza parlor on the menu, but before she can make the call, there's a big crash in the living room and we both rush out the kitchen to find out what happened.

In the living room, there's Gee, standing up and frowning at the TV. I'm not surprised that he went from being sound asleep to wide-awake, because he does that a lot, even before the stroke, but it is startling to see his tray knocked over—which was the crash—and the remote control on the floor broken into pieces.

"Daddy!" Mama yells. "What in the world is going on?"

It seems obvious to me what happened. Gee threw the remote at the TV.

Malcolm bursts out of his room. "What was that?" he shouts from upstairs.

John Wayne is still in the middle of a shouting match with someone.

Gee raises his arm and points at the TV and makes a sort of coughing, barking noise. It sounds a lot like *no* to me, and I go over and turn off the TV. I'm glad to see the remote didn't crack the screen.

"If you wanted the channel changed, why didn't you just say so?" Mama grumbles, and well, after that, I can't help but laugh. It is too ridiculous. And the more I laugh, the more I can't stop, and Malcolm starts, and then even Mama joins in.

And I'm telling you, those belly laughs feel so good. It has been a long time since we all had a good laugh together. Gee isn't laughing, but his eyes are twinkling. I guess Gee really is done with John Wayne.

I wait for Aubrey outside of history in the morning. I can't wait to tell him what happened.

"Who knew TV screens were so tough?" I ask. And the laughter comes right back, and Aubrey laughs with me.

"You think he's tired of Westerns?" Aubrey asks.

"Hah!" I say. "John Wayne, yes, but Westerns? Never." The idea of Gee not watching Westerns starts me laughing again.

But I'm not laughing at lunch when Aubrey tells me he and his mom are going out of town for the weekend.

"My mom wants to check out a couple of restaurants in San Diego. We're driving down right after school. It'll be fun. We're not coming back until Sunday night!" He says it like him being gone for two whole days is no big deal.

"But . . ." I don't know what to say. By the time he comes back, we'll only have two days left.

"Oh, don't worry, I'll still work on my side of our debate," Aubrey says, totally not understanding.

I put my lunch back in the bag. I've lost my appetite.

In English, Mr. Humphries shows us a clip from a movie called *The Great Debaters*. It's strange seeing students so excited to give speeches. It's hard for me to believe the movie is based on a true story.

I try to think of how I can make Aubrey forgive me after Wednesday. Speech Day. Maybe if he truly understood how completely impossible it is for me to stand in front of people so exposed? But people don't understand something they can't feel. What's real for me doesn't seem real for anyone else. Aubrey thinks I'm just nervous. It's way more than that. And I don't think there's a way for me to convince him.

Two days is all I'll have.

After school, I wait for him. I want to say bye before he leaves for San Diego.

He doesn't come out right away, and as the minutes tick by, I start to get nervous. Should I keep waiting? Maybe he got held up in his sixth period. Maybe he already left.

People pass me, and I start to inch toward the line of bushes in front of the school. I am trying to disappear and can't quite manage it. I'm out of practice.

Then Aubrey blows out the big front doors of the school, and I'm so relieved it's embarrassing.

"You waited for me!" he shouts.

My face heats up as people turn to look at us, but I shrug like it's no big deal. "I figured I'd say bye."

"Del!" he says with that ginormous smile, bright enough to light up the whole block. "Hey, there's my mom!" He points to a gray SUV that's just pulled up. "Come and say hi."

I slowly walk with him to the car. Even though I've met his mom, I still feel awkward going up to the car like this.

"Hi, Mrs. Banks," I tell her shyly.

"Oh, shoot, call me Ellen!" she says, beaming at me, and I nod, even though I know I won't do it. Mama doesn't like me calling adults by their first names. Mrs. Banks's hair is free from the bun she was wearing last time and flows in long waves. The blue streak is hidden away.

"We're hitting the road!" she says, sounding excited. Gee would probably really like her.

Aubrey starts to climb into the car, and my shoulders slump. For the first time in my life, I'm not looking forward to the weekend.

"Hop in," Mrs. Banks says. "We'll give you a ride home."

It's only about five more minutes of Aubrey time, but I want it, and so I slide into the back seat.

"Thanks," I say, and my voice comes out a little breathless and excited, as if we are about to set off on a fantastic voyage.

Aubrey and his mom joke around about stuff, including what type of food they'll eat when they get to San Diego. Mrs. Banks really wants to focus on Mexican food and seafood, but Aubrey wants Italian.

"But it's San Diego!" Mrs. Banks says. "The whole point is to get things they're known for."

I enjoy the bantering back and forth. Mama and I are never like this.

We get to my house way too soon.

"I'll text you!" Aubrey shouts out the window before they drive off.

I grip the strap of my bag tight and watch them drive away.

When I get inside, my auntie Jackie is already in the kitchen starting to get things going for the fish fry.

"Your mama told me to make sure I keep you away from the flour," she says. And even though I know she's just kidding, it irritates me, and I stomp my foot like a two-year-old.

"I know how to hold a bag!" I say. Auntie Jackie's eyes go wide, but before she can say anything, I spin on my heel and rush out the kitchen. Gee looks at me expectantly, but I'm in no mood to deliver mail today, and I head upstairs.

I need Malcolm's music.

I need something hard and pounding and angry, but there's no sound coming from Malcolm's room, and when I knock on his door, he doesn't answer. I creak the door open, but Malcolm isn't there.

It's like the whole world is letting me down.

48

JUST A DREAM

I put two big black Xs over Saturday and Sunday on my friendship calendar and stare at Monday and Tuesday. What's the point? There's nothing Aubrey and I can do for two days that will be epic-friendship material. Nothing I can hold on to that will make all the long friendless days after okay.

I get into comfy sweats and a too-small T-shirt my dad gave me from one of his movies and climb into bed. I hear the front door open and close a bunch of times as my aunties and uncles arrive. Mama will drag me downstairs once she gets home from work, but right now, I don't want to see anyone or have to talk to anybody.

I pull my covers over my head. They almost drown out the laughter and commotion from my family.

When I open my eyes, at first I don't hear anything. And then I hear it. The *ba-thunk, ba-thunk* of a basketball outside.

I sit straight up. It's all been a dream! Malcolm never left. Gee didn't have a stroke. Everything's okay! Even as I notice that the ball outside doesn't sound quite right, I try to hold on to the idea of a long, awful dream.

I push back the covers and hop out of bed. I see my clothes from yesterday in a heap instead of neatly put away. So no one came up to get me last night? They forgot all about me and just let me sleep through the fish fry? I shake my head hard. That couldn't have happened. It must not be real.

"Dream," I whisper to no one.

I shove my feet into shoes without socks and hustle downstairs and out the front door, chanting, "Dream, dream," the whole way.

As I burst out the front door, my last "dream" dies on my lips. I bet this is how a hummingbird feels when it flies smack into a picture window.

Malcolm is sitting in the driveway, his head between his knees, his brace on the ground next to him and his crutches tossed on the grass. His basketball has rolled into the gutter, resting in the runoff from someone's sprinklers and a pile of leaves.

I wipe my face off fast and run to get the ball. "You want me to rebound for you?" I ask, trying to sound chipper. As if I don't even notice Malcolm looking defeated.

Malcolm slowly raises his head, and if I didn't know my brother better, I'd swear he'd been crying. He looks at the ball in my hands, then at his basketball hoop. He takes a big breath and gets up on his feet, grimacing as he does. He picks up his brace and straps it back on. "Yeah," he says. "Yeah, sure."

I toss him the ball and he does a layup, nice and easy. He dribbles out to what would be about the free-throw line, taking limping steps, and thumps the ball hard on the ground and then starts dribbling between his legs. Around and through. Around and through. Threading a needle.

"Coach Eric called me. Talking 'bout how I need to stop feeling sorry for myself." Coach Eric was Malcolm's high school coach. He hollered a lot at the games, but all the players loved him. I wouldn't like being shouted at. Maybe it's easier to take when you're winning almost all the time.

Malcolm takes a shot, and it goes neatly through the hoop without touching the rim. "He thinks he knows everything. But I'm not feeling *sorry*. I'm pissed."

I run over and get the ball and bring it back to Malcolm.

He takes it with a frown. "I bet Mama told him to call me. Like it's her life and not mine. People need to step off."

"But everyone just wants you to get better," I say in a shallow voice.

"What? I have a bad cold? The flu? Nobody can fix this for me, Jenae!" He points to his knee. "Maybe *people* should leave me alone and let me figure my own stuff out."

I don't know what to say. It's like Malcolm somehow knows about me texting Rox about him, but I can't stop texting her now. Aren't you supposed to help people you care about?

Malcolm tosses the ball up and catches and turns it around in his hands like he's looking for a sweet spot. Then he surprises me by giving a small half smile. "Of course, when I said all that to Coach, he said get outside and shoot." Malcolm shakes his head like Coach Eric is so ridiculous. "Reminded me of when we weren't playing as good as we were supposed to and he'd get on us. Tell us to get mad, but to use it." Malcolm starts dribbling the ball slowly and keeps looking over at the basketball rim.

"You want to shoot some more?" I ask. "Or play some one-on-one?" I can't really play basketball very well, but Malcolm and I used to joke around, playing together. Sometimes he'd lift me up high so I could make a shot.

Malcolm raises his eyebrows, the way he used to do when he was about to do something fancy on the court. "Check," he says, and tosses the ball at me.

49

FROZEN

It isn't until we go inside a little while later, when the lingering scent of overheated oil and fish sting my nose, that I remember last night. Remember being forgotten. No matter how yummy the food was, it seems like Mama or one of my aunties or Malcolm would've said, "Where's Jenae?" But no one did. Maybe they have gotten too used to me being invisible.

And even though it's been my choice to go unnoticed, my feelings are hurt. Especially since my idea of hanging out with Aubrey this weekend is ruined. I wish I could go back to believing it had just been a bad dream.

Malcolm settles on the couch. "You mind getting me some ice?" he asks.

That's a sure sign he's in pain, so I hustle to the kitchen to put some ice in a gallon-size baggie. The kitchen isn't as clean as when Mama and I clean up together after a fish fry. Did the family pitch in? Did Mama even think about it normally just being me and her?

I yank open the freezer and dig a hand into the ice tray.

Clump by clump I fill the baggie. The ice makes my hand super cold. So cold, it hurts. I rub my hand fast over my sweats, to erase the pain. I think of Astrid Dane staying underneath the ice for so long. It never occurred to me that maybe being frozen like that might've hurt.

You'd think ice would numb all the pain away instead of making something hurt even worse.

When I bring Malcolm the baggie full of ice, he asks me, "You hanging out with your little friend today?"

The question pokes at me. Gets under my skin. Like I have one of Astrid's ghosts inside me pushing to get out. "He's not my friend, I mean, not really. I barely know him." I hang my head and examine the grass clinging to my dew-drenched shoes.

"And he doesn't know me," I add under my breath.

"Don't do that, Jenae," Malcolm says, his voice sharp.

"What?"

"Throw away something good."

"You mean like you're doing with school?" I probably wouldn't have asked that if Malcolm wasn't making me mad. Like he already knows it's my fault me and Aubrey aren't going to stay friends.

Malcolm drums his fingers on his good knee. His face is stormy, and I think he's going to say something mean back to me, but then all he says is "Touché." Then he adjusts the bag of ice, leans back, and closes his eyes. "Okay, worst thing. What was it?"

I don't want to play. It seems like I have too many worst

things. But after a few seconds I say, "Aubrey leaving for the weekend."

"Oh," Malcolm says. "But he's coming back. Quit trippin'."

"I'm not," I say, even though I am.

I'm tripping so hard that if I was the sort of person to throw something, I would. Why couldn't Aubrey have just left me alone? I wasn't bothering anyone. I was fine. He should've picked someone else to sit with at lunch. He should've picked someone else to partner with. You can't just force yourself on somebody. Especially somebody who doesn't want anybody.

50

NOT A VERY GOOD ARGUMENT

Later that day, my phone buzzes with a message from Aubrey. It's a picture of a plate of shrimp tacos. I don't answer. What do I care about tacos? A little bit later, he texts:

Don't they look delicious?

I guess they do, but I don't feel like talking about tacos or anything else really, and I delete the message without answering. He keeps texting. Two more pictures of food. One message about the Astrid Dane graphic novel he bought and a video of his mom asleep and snoring. (With that one he also sent a laughing emoji.) His very last message says:

Hello? Hello? Checking 1, 2, 3!

I don't answer any of them. I yank the friendship calendar off my wall. It was a stupid idea anyway.

And I don't worry about it, not really, until Monday rolls around. My stomach feels nervous and achy the whole way to school. It doesn't help at all seeing the usual groups of protesters outside of school.

I head to first period feeling as if my stomach is shriveled like a raisin.

"Hey," Aubrey says when he sees me. "You really need to remember to charge your phone."

I stare at him. I guess in his world people don't get mad. Don't ignore messages. I can imagine his mother giving him this solid reason for not hearing from me. I'm a typical kid who doesn't remember to charge my phone. And it would be so easy to pretend that was really what happened and slide back into friendship. Two days is better than nothing, right? "My phone was charged. I got your messages." I shrug. "Just didn't have anything to say."

Aubrey's eyes open wide for a second, but then he nods. "Sway."

"No one says that here," I say, with as much anger as I can muster. I slide past him into class and try desperately to disappear. I push hard into the molded plastic of my chair, willing it to absorb my energy.

But it's no use. I'm stuck here, and when Aubrey settles into the chair next to me, he reaches over and touches my arm and says, "Sorry."

That just makes me feel worse, and I pull my arm away.

By lunch, I feel more numb than angry. The day is just a day. It's the way the days will go from here on out, and so instead of going to the cafeteria like I had sort of maybe planned, I go over to our regular spot by the container and settle on the grass. Aubrey joins me a few minutes later.

"Hey," he says, just like this morning, but it's not just like this morning, because this time his greeting is soft and careful. It is creeping-up-on-a-moth careful.

"Hey," I say, not angry, but not friendly either.

He sits next to me and starts pulling out stuff from his lunch. Prosciutto. Melon. Fancy crackers.

It's exactly the type of lunch I would've packed for myself, and my mouth waters. I didn't pack anything today.

He looks at my empty hands, the empty space around me, and holds out the container of melon. "Want some?"

I don't bother hesitating. I just grab a chunk and let the sweetness of the melon fill my mouth and warm up all the frozen bits of me. When he shakes the baggie of prosciutto, I take a piece and let the saltiness of the meat blend with the melon. It's delicious. "Thanks," I say.

"Have you ever been to San Diego?" he asks, over a mouthful of melon.

I roll my eyes. "Uh, yeah," I say sarcastically. "Of course I have." The truth is, I've only been there once, and that was when I was small. Mama and my dad were still together. I barely remember it.

"The best Comic-Con is there."

"I *know*," I say. "I'm actually from California." I don't say it mean, more teasing, more like a friend would talk to another friend. At least how I imagine they would.

Aubrey chuckles. "It would be so cool to go. Especially if the creators of Astrid Dane had a booth."

"Yeah," I say, and take another piece of melon.

Aubrey and I sit side by side with the sun hitting our faces, chewing his lunch and letting the shouts and laughter from the lunch tables drift around us.

"It's funny when you think how it wasn't that long ago," I say, really talking to myself.

"What wasn't?"

"The whole Sylvia Mendez thing. The people who didn't want her to go to their school. Do you think that's what they didn't want?" I point across the field. "All different races hanging out together?"

Aubrey shrugs. "Nothing about it makes sense to me," he says.

"Not a very good argument," I say before I can stop to think about it.

When the bell rings, Aubrey gets up and offers me his hand, and I grip it. He pulls me up harder than he should, and I stumble to my feet and almost face-plant.

"Watch it!" I say, but I'm laughing, and Aubrey laughs too, and that's how we walk to English, both cracking up over something that wasn't even funny.

51

RESPECTING HISTORY

But when we get to class, I start to feel nervous. I don't know why. Aubrey and I aren't on the schedule Mr. Humphries posted on the whiteboard. Still, just knowing the speeches start today is making me sweaty, and my stomach cramps. Not like period cramps. This is different. More like sharp rocks are inside me.

Mr. Humphries takes attendance, and then we head to the auditorium. On the way, we're joined by a small group of eighth graders. Some of the debate club, I guess, and Aubrey says hi to all of them. Even though they act like they don't know who he is, it still annoys me, and I slow down so we're not walking next to each other. He doesn't even notice.

Mr. Humphries is holding a clipboard and takes a seat behind all of us—probably so he can make sure we're all paying attention.

"Remember what I told you last week," he says to the backs of our heads. "The most important thing is managing your breath. Breathe deep before you begin. And don't forget to take a breath before you run out of air. Don't talk too fast.

Talk slower than you think you should." Then he calls the first set of partners.

The first argument is about school lunches, and one side argues they need to taste better, and the other side says they need to be healthy. They don't seem nervous at all; it's like they don't even care a bunch of eighth graders are watching too. All I can think is, I would rather die than get up on that stage. And I'm not even kidding.

Dawn Hernandez and her partner take the stage after the first team is done. She obviously got dressed up for this. She looks so pretty in her purple dress with tiny turquoise flowers. Her hair is in a big loose bun, and she stands perfectly straight while she talks about how schools should make students wear uniforms. I wish she was Aubrey's partner. I think she would've liked talking about Sylvia Mendez and how important the name change is. I think it might mean more to her than me. It means a lot to me too, but I know it's not the same. Maybe I should talk to her to get her perspective.

The thought makes me dig my fingernails into my hand. I'm not giving the speech. I don't need to talk to her about anything.

Six teams are scheduled for each day, and after each pair goes, Aubrey nudges me and whispers which side he thinks won. I agree with him each time.

After the last team gives their speeches, Mr. Humphries goes up onstage to congratulate all the people who went today. "Thank you, everyone, for getting us off to a great start. I hope you all were listening. You'll be writing a short essay on one of the topics you heard."

When everyone groans, he chuckles. "Oh, didn't I mention that?" Mr. Humphries thinks he is a riot factory.

"We'll do a lot better than the groups today," Aubrey whispers to me. "You're practicing, right? You think you have a good argument for why we shouldn't respect history?" he asks, still whispering.

"Some history doesn't need to be respected," I say. I forget to whisper, and Mr. Humphries looks over at us.

"Save your arguments for Wednesday," Mr. Humphries tells me and Aubrey. Then he claps his hands, releasing everyone to sixth period.

As we start to file out, Aubrey says, "So that's the point you're gonna make? We shouldn't respect John Wayne?"

"You think we should?" I ask.

"But a person isn't bad just because they say *one* bad thing, right? Or only do one bad thing?"

It depends on what the bad thing is, I think, but I say, "No, not even. Besides, I don't think it was just *one* bad thing." I adjust the strap of my book bag. "But that's not the point. I think the name should change so that we *can* respect history. Sylvia Mendez is more important than a movie star. Being in movies doesn't make you so great." I'm not sure if I'm talking about John Wayne or my dad.

Aubrey nods at me. "Not bad. Not bad at all. I'll make a debater out of you yet."

No, you won't, I think.

In the hallway, I tell Dawn what a good job she did. She looks at me shocked that I'm talking to her, and honestly, I'm just as shocked myself.

"Thanks," she says. "I'm looking forward to yours."

"It's going to be del!" Aubrey shouts, and I almost trip over my feet.

"Del?" Dawn says, and I rush away, not wanting to see Aubrey start being friends with someone new.

52

A THANKSGIVING SANDWICH

The next morning, I make a special lunch. It's plenty big too. Enough for me and Aubrey. A farewell lunch.

On the way to school, Mama sings along to the radio as if she's the only one in the car. I wish she'd notice I'm feeling down. She told me things would be different in junior high, and she's right, but I'm sure this isn't what she meant.

Even though I don't know what I'd say, I wish she'd ask me what's wrong. I wish she'd ask me *something*. I feel like I'm just watching myself. Floating above my own body like a balloon.

I get out of the car and bounce along, feeling the tug of a string.

Aubrey talks to me in history, and I watch myself answer. We laugh at something, but I don't know what.

At lunch, I see myself give him his sandwich, and he turns it around and around in amazement.

"This is the best sandwich I've ever seen," he says, and I know it's the truth. Miles of turkey, a smear of goat cheese, crisp butter lettuce, a heavy dollop of cranberry sauce. A thanksgiving sandwich.

"Thanks," Aubrey says worshipfully, and I want to tell him I'm the one who should be thanking him. For the past two weeks. But I can't make myself say the words. This is our last day. Our very last day, and I can't make myself enjoy it. Not really.

He pulls an Astrid Dane graphic novel out of his bag, and we sit side by side flipping the pages, and I watch and watch and watch. An image of Astrid Dane fills one whole page, and she looks like she's staring right at me, and I draw closer and almost make it back into myself, but then Aubrey turns the page.

When the bell rings, we get up and head straight to the auditorium like Mr. Humphries told us to yesterday.

Our class files in, and I see several eighth graders are already there, talking to Mr. Humphries. After we're in our seats, the door opens, and Ms. Garcia's class comes in.

"Great! You were able to join us," Mr. Humphries calls out. "My students," he says to us. "Ms. Garcia's class is taking time out of their busy schedule to watch your speeches. You know when we do competitions, the rooms are packed with people."

Why did Mr. Humphries invite even more people? Why would he take something so bad and make it worse? All these people. Staring. Waiting to hear some dumb speeches about stuff no one cares about.

Mr. Humphries must feel my worry, because he says,

"When Ms. Garcia heard how great everyone did yesterday, she asked if her class could watch and get an idea of how to deliver an effective argument." He smiles kindly at me, and I work hard not to stick my tongue out at him.

I fold and unfold my legs. I wish the auditorium were dark. A girl almost sits right on top of me, and Aubrey points her to the next seat over. Maybe I'm really not here.

When the first set of partners goes up, I feel nervous for them. The boy, Jeremy, drops his note cards and full-on panic settles into my neck and shoulders. It takes him a few minutes to pick up the cards because his hands are shaking a little. He must be nervous. Part of me hopes he won't be able to do it. Maybe if one other person bails on giving a speech, Mr. Humphries will realize that for some of us, what he's asked us to do is impossible.

But Jeremy starts his speech, looking at his note cards the entire time even though Mr. Humphries told us how we're supposed to look up. Jeremy's voice wavers a little and he's talking pretty low, but he finishes. When everyone claps, Jeremy looks so surprised, it's almost funny, and then his partner gives her speech, they both make comments about each other's points, and then they get to leave the stage.

All the other partners scheduled for today deliver their speeches. You can tell who did research and who didn't. But no one looks like they might die. I feel like I might die, and I don't even have to go up onstage today.

"Good job, everyone," Mr. Humphries says, just as the bell rings. "Thank you, Ms. Garcia's class. You were an excellent audience. Be ready, Wednesday partners. Mrs. Park's class is going to come tomorrow."

Aubrey grins at me like he's so excited for Wednesday. Like he actually wants to get up on that stage and stand in front of everyone with them staring, and wondering, and judging. Like the words will just come out easily and make sense instead of a horrible garble. He grins like not only does he believe all that but like he thinks *I* believe it too. And I realize he doesn't know me at all. And I float far away.

53

THE ENEMY

It's our very last day of friendship, so when I see Aubrey after school and he says, "No consorting with the enemy," instead of asking if he can come over, my heart dips all the way to my toes.

"Besides," he adds, "I have a lot of work to do if I'm going to beat you tomorrow. It's going to be so great getting to be in the debate club!" Aubrey sounds so positive. He swings his Astrid Dane bag into my Astrid Dane bag, grins at me, and then heads in the opposite direction of where I'm going. As he gets farther away, I want to call him back to tell him it would be better if we worked together. At least we'd have a little more time. But I also want to shout that I'm sorry he won't be in the club. I zip my lips closed. Our friendship is over, and I might as well accept that right now.

Across the street, the crowd is big and loud. "Save John Wayne!" someone shouts, as if instead of a name change people want to close the school.

We must be getting close to the school board meeting,

because the crowd is not only bigger, it seems more intense.

On my walk home, I force one foot in front of the other. After what Malcolm said about Mama having Coach Eric call him, it feels doubly wrong to be texting Rox, but last night I saw a list of college classes on the computer desktop. Malcolm must be thinking about going back. And maybe that means even if he doesn't want help, he actually does need it. If I stop now, what if he goes back to feeling down and not wanting to do anything? *You break it, you buy it.* I have to finish what I started and really and truly fix him.

I pull out my phone and type a text message to Rox. Telling her he said he doesn't care about school anymore. That he said he doesn't care about anything.

It's all a lie, and I stare at the message for a long time before finally pressing send.

Rox texts me back right away.

He's just scared. Don't worry. We've been talking and I think he'll be okay. He's supposed to come over. I'll call him and make sure.

Suddenly, my feet feel lighter and I just about glide all the way home. Everything else might be messed up, but at least I've done this one good thing.

When I turn the corner of our street, I can see someone on the front porch, but it's not until I get closer that I can tell it's Malcolm. And it's not until I'm really close that I see the anger written all over his face.

"What were you thinking?" he yells at me.

I clutch my bag tight and take a step back, away from the blast of anger.

"You can't just mess with people's lives! You can't go around texting folks trying to make something happen! What's wrong with you?" He's yelling so loud, I'm sure all the neighbors can hear.

"Malcolm, I was only trying to h—"

"Help?" He holds his phone out. "You think you're *helping* by texting my ex? Making her feel sorry for me? Making me think . . . You didn't help anybody!" He turns around and goes inside, slamming the door so hard behind him, I'm shocked it doesn't crack.

My phone vibrates, and I don't want to look but I do anyway. It's Rox. Saying she doesn't understand why I told her things that weren't true. And lots of sad face emojis. I want to explain that most of what I texted her wasn't a *complete* lie. It was what I thought was true, or at least mostly. And that I'm really sorry. But I'm pretty sure she doesn't want to see any more texts from me.

I force myself up the steps and into the house. I'm afraid to see Malcolm, but when I get inside, he's gone upstairs; the music blasting from his room is angry and lava hot.

Even with all the commotion, Gee is asleep in his chair, and I don't know what to do. I messed up *everything*.

54

EVERY SINGLE THING

I walk to the kitchen and pull out things for dinner.

I know it was wrong for me to text Rox behind Malcolm's back, but I'm sure it made him happy hearing from her. Why is he so mad about it?

I feel my phone buzzing, and I don't want to look because it's probably Rox again, but it's not.

It's my dad.

Sorry baby. Something came up. Have to fly to New York. I won't be able to pick you up tomorrow after all.

I stare and stare and stare. I know there's not one solitary thing I can say that will make him change his plans. And even though it was a lie I told, him saying he can't come after I told him I needed him to hurts so bad, it's like having a whole mouthful of rotten teeth.

Every single thing is ruined.

I head upstairs and try to do homework, but instead I wonder and wonder and wonder. What am I going to do?

"Astrid," I whisper. "What would you do?"

The answer comes so suddenly, I swear Astrid whispered it in my ear. Mama will be mad, but if it's a choice between having my hide tanned or giving a speech, I'd rather get the spanking. I get into sweats and burrow into bed.

55
SO SICK

In the morning, I sneak downstairs and take a little bit of mustard and rub it on my face. Not so much that it's obvious and cakey, but just enough to know I don't look exactly right. I get the heating pad from the closet and take it to my room and turn it on high. And then I get back into bed. The mustard starts burning and it smells. Mama is never going to fall for it. I start rubbing the mustard off and it gets in my eyes. OUCH!

I dash to the bathroom and scrub my face. My eyes are burning and red. I look terrible.

Good. I climb into bed with the heading pad on my chest and wait.

It doesn't take too long. When I don't go downstairs after Mama calls me a second time, I hear her marching up the stairs, and I quickly stash the heating pad out of sight. A few seconds later, Mama flings my door open.

"Didn't you hear—" Her voice breaks off when she sees me still in bed. "What's wrong with you? Why aren't you up?" She comes over and looks at me, then puts her hand on my forehead. I'm really glad I don't still smell like mustard.

"Oh, Lord, you're burning up," she says. "And you don't look good at all." She sighs loudly. "How do you feel?"

"Like I might throw up," I say. Vomit is something Mama would rather avoid.

"Well, okay, then. I guess I better call the school. I hope this is just a one-day thing. You can't be getting behind. Not in junior high." She shakes her head, and I so want to tell her she doesn't have to worry. That I'll only be sick one day. But I stay quiet and look as mournful and queasy as I can.

She stares at me for a minute, and I can tell she's a little suspicious. I cough. I've never stayed home sick from school. Not once. I have a whole stack of perfect attendance records. Which is probably why she says, "All right, then," and heads out of my room.

I actually feel like I might really throw up. What I'm doing is horribly wrong.

A little while later, Mama taps on my door and opens it slowly when I don't answer. She comes over and kisses me on the forehead. "Let Malcolm know if you need anything, okay?" she says, and I nod sadly and close my eyes.

I don't think Malcolm would do a thing for me. I hear Mama's soft steps cross the floor and then the click of my door closing. I don't open my eyes until I hear her car pull out of the driveway.

★ ★ ★

After first period, my phone buzzes and I know it's Aubrey.

Where are you? Do you have a doctor's appointment or something?

I don't answer.

A little while later he texts again.

Okay, well I'll see you at lunch.

But before lunchtime rolls around, he must've figured it out, because he texts:

You have to come!

I head downstairs. Malcolm is in the kitchen frying some bacon.

"Hey," I say softly.

"You want something to eat?" he asks, not turning around.

I shake my head. My stomach feels hard and tight.

When I don't answer out loud, Malcolm turns to look at me. "You look whooped," he says.

"Thanks," I say.

"Sorry," we both say at the same time. Malcolm shakes his head at me.

"I shouldn't have yelled at you, but you can't do stuff like that."

"I know," I say. "But I hurt you, Malcolm, and I had to fix it. I had to."

"What are you talking about?" He takes the bacon out of the skillet and then cracks an egg into the hot bacon grease. I watch him while trying to figure out how to answer his question. He glances at me over his shoulder.

"I did it," I whisper. "I made you get hurt."

"*What?*" He turns back to his food for a second and slides his egg out of the skillet onto a plate, then turns around to face me. He looks confused and sort of annoyed. "So you sent some bad mojo at me? You *made* me fall? Made my knee snap all apart? Are you serious right now?" He chuckles in a dry way.

Yes, I want to say. Yes. Yes. Yes. "Malcolm, I—I just missed you so much. And I wanted you to come back, but I didn't mean for you to get hurt. I didn't know that was going to happen."

Malcolm takes a bite of bacon and chews slowly. After he swallows, he says, "Jenae," and waits for me to look at him.

"I got injured playing ball, just like what happens to tons of players. You know how common this type of injury is?" he asks, pointing to his knee. "It didn't have anything to do with you."

It's okay that he doesn't believe me—it still feels as if a boulder is lifted from my arms. It's been so heavy carrying that around. "I shouldn't have texted Rox," I say.

"No, you shouldn't have," Malcolm says. "I know you were trying to help. But it's my life, got it?" He gobbles down the rest of his breakfast, watching me until I nod. "I'm not dumb. I can figure things out on my own."

"Okay," I say.

"Cool, or what's that new word? Sway? It's sway," he says, and comes over and gives my shoulder a squeeze.

Gee shambles into the kitchen. Even though he's not walking super steady, he's dressed in slacks and an ironed buttoned-up shirt. It's strange to see, because since he's been home from the hospital, he's been wearing old beige chinos and one of his million Hawaiian shirts.

"You going somewhere, old man?" Malcolm asks, and then laughs. "My bad. All your regular clothes are dirty, huh? Mama told me to do your laundry. Sorry, I'll get to it today."

It looks good to see Gee dressed up, like he's all better, but sort of sad too. Like he's only wearing a costume.

"Mornin', Gee," I say softly, as if, if I talk too loud, this version of Gee will evaporate and he'll go back to looking frail.

Malcolm makes Gee a bacon-and-egg sandwich and guides Gee out to the living room. I hear the television turn on, and the volume is so loud, I can tell it's a Western, but I know even without checking it's not a John Wayne one.

With him appearing so much healthier than he's been since he came home from the hospital, I'm surprised that Gee's doing his same routine. "I'll wash his clothes," I tell Malcolm. I bet it's not comfortable wearing stiff pants and a shirt when all you're doing is lounging around watching TV.

"Thanks," Malcolm says. "You feeling okay?"

I shrug.

"Reason I'm asking is Coach Naz is in town. He's recruiting Johnny Knox—you know that kid getting all the press?"

I haven't heard of him, but I don't follow sports like Malcolm does.

"He had asked if I could meet him for lunch. I guess they got all excited hearing I was thinking about coming back." He actually looks embarrassed, and I'm surprised. Doesn't he know how good he is? How much they'd want him back even if there was just a small chance he could still play?

"Rox and I have been . . . you know, sort of talking, and she was pushing me to meet with him, but I wasn't going to. . . ." Malcolm's eyes drift away. He stares at the corner of the room. "Anyway, since you're here, maybe I should, you know? Coach Eric was right about me being sorry for myself. And it's not like I can just sit around at home for the rest of my life."

I nod fast at him. It's almost as if I can see him right on the edge teetering. All he needs is one tiny push in the right direction.

"But I didn't want to leave Gee alone, and if you're not up to it—"

"You should go!" I almost shout. "I'm fine." That's too close to admitting my lie about being sick. "I mean, not fine, but you know, I can watch Gee."

"Maybe I better not," he says. "You're sick, and I don't know if I even want to see this dude."

Just one little push. "Go," I say.

He looks down at his brace, then back at me, and then he surprises me by smiling. "Yeah, I guess. I know whatever else happens, I still want to get my degree. Maybe I'll go into sports medicine or business. I sort of like numbers."

"Me too!" I say, smiling at him. He's going back! I'm sure of it. And I feel happy but also sort of sad.

A thought bubbles up inside of me, and I push it out to the universe. I think it as hard as I can.

THANK YOU.

Gee used to tell me all the time you can't always just ask for things. Sometimes you have to show you're grateful for what you've got.

I join Gee in the living room and try not to pay attention to the day ticking away.

Malcolm leaves around eleven thirty. First, he asks me, "You sure about this?"

I look at Gee, point to the TV, and shrug. "Piece of cake."

When the door closes behind Malcolm, Gee turns and glares at me.

I pretend it has nothing to do with me not being at school. With me letting down the only real friend I've ever had. Probably will ever have. "Watch the movie, Gee," I grumble, and he turns back to the TV.

At lunch my phone vibrates again.

Come on Jenae. Don't do this. You know how bad I want to be in debate club.

Please.

I could get dressed and run to school. I would make it for fifth period. I have all the information for my side of the speech. I stare at the back of Gee's head. He would be fine. I could give the speech and come right back. My throat tightens. I imagine the auditorium. And all the people staring. Watching me. Seeing me. My tongue fills my whole mouth, choking me.

The debate club is really for eighth graders. Aubrey can be in the dumb club all next year. And be friends with all the debate kids. Kids who are like him. Loud. And actually *want* to be seen.

I'm sure when Aubrey imagined being at a regular school, he didn't just want to make one friend. He probably saw himself with a whole slew of them. Instead, he got stuck with me.

I turn off my phone. I set it on the couch.

"I . . . I'm going upstairs, Gee," I say. The television is so loud, I doubt Gee even heard me, or maybe he's already dozed off. Slowly, I make my way upstairs, to my room, back into bed.

I stare at the ceiling thinking I am probably the worst person alive.

56
GONE MISSING

My eyes fly open, and I sit up. I hadn't meant to fall asleep. I have no clue what time it is. I left my phone downstairs.

Downstairs.

I should hear the TV blasting, but the house is silent. I leap out of bed and race down the stairs, but I know. I just know. There's a special silence of an empty house.

Gee's not in his chair.

"Gee," I call out. "Gee!" I run into the kitchen. He's not there. Since his stroke, he's been staying in the downstairs bedroom so he doesn't have to deal with the stairs, and I check there. "Gee?" I knock, but when he doesn't answer, I creak open the door. Empty.

I run upstairs. Maybe he decided to go up to his actual room. The one he and Nana June shared. "Gee!" I don't bother knocking this time but just yank the door open. He's not there either.

My heart is pumping so hard, it's filling up my ears, and I can't hear and I can't think. Where is he?

I check the backyard. Nothing.

I come back inside and stand in the kitchen for a second, trying not to panic. Maybe he left a note! But I check the pad next to his chair, and it's as blank as it has always been. I have to call Mama. My chest squeezes tight, but I head back out to the living room, and grab my phone off the couch. I have lots of missed messages from Aubrey, but I don't read them. It's three forty-five. I left Gee alone for hours. I'm sweating as I start to punch in Mama's number. I don't want to call her. She'll be so mad.

Our mail hits the entryway floor with a loud *thunk*.

Mail. Mail! He's probably out delivering mail. Relief floods me, and I can breathe again.

I run to the door so fast I almost slip on the pile of catalogs and magazines. I can see someone at the door, and my relief grows. He's back.

But when I open the door, ready to give Gee a piece of my mind for scaring me like that, the scolding words burn and die in my throat. It's not Gee standing there.

It's Aubrey.

57

NOT ANYWHERE

My mouth opens and shuts. What can I say? It's Wednesday, and that means me and Aubrey are officially not friends anymore and it's too much to try and talk about. Besides, my grandfather is missing. I push past Aubrey, closing the front door behind me. When I hit the sidewalk, I look up and down the street. I don't see Gee.

Aubrey follows me.

"How could you do that to me?" he shouts at me. "It was *important*. You didn't even care."

I don't have time for this, but I turn and face him anyway. "I *did* care, but I told you I couldn't do it. You should've listened to me! I told you to pick a different partner."

His face tightens into a grimace. "I wanted to be partners with *you*. You're my friend. Friends are supposed to be there for each other. I never asked you for anything except for this one thing!"

"That's not true! You asked for stuff all the time."

"Like what, Jenae?"

"To be friends! For me to be like you!" I shout. If Aubrey knew me at all, he should've known he was asking for the hardest thing.

"I have to go," I say. I know if I tell him Gee is missing, he'll offer to look with me. We could run down the street together, or we could split up and he would look one way while I look the other, and somehow as we were looking, we'd be fixing things and Aubrey and I could be friends again, but I don't do it.

Aubrey reaches forward like he's going to grab my arm, and I step back.

I turn and run down the street. Toward Tía Rosalie's house. I bet that's where Gee is. Having another cup of that delicious cocoa. I expect to hear the pounding of Aubrey's feet chasing after me, but I don't, and when I get to her walkway I force myself not to turn around to see if he's still standing on the sidewalk.

I don't want him to be.

I want him to be.

I push the doorbell over and over. "Tía Rosalie!" I holler, and start pounding on her door. "Tía!" She doesn't answer. I'm not sure how long I stand there. Just long enough for a boy with flaming-red hair to disappear. I start running again.

As I run, I check each porch. Even the house with the dandelions as tall as me, and the screens ripped and flapping in the slight breeze. But Gee's not anywhere. All those hours. He could've walked over a mile, over two. Why isn't Malcolm back? Didn't he say he wouldn't be gone long? How could he have just left me? I keep looking, even while I remind myself this isn't Malcolm's fault. It's all mine.

And I know I can't possibly wait any longer. With shaking fingers, I punch Mama's number into my phone.

58

A TERRIBLE THING

Mama's voice is razor-sharp as she tells me to wait for her at home; that she's going to report Gee missing at the police station.

I slowly walk back to the house, rechecking the houses I've already checked. My legs feel like they weigh a thousand pounds, and the air presses against me like wet concrete.

Mama is always sharing with me and Malcolm the police notifications she gets at home, alerting the neighborhood about robberies and chain snatchings and reckless drivers and at-risk missing persons. Now that person is going to be Gee.

When I get home, I check the computer and see the police have already sent out the email alert. There's a picture of Gee Mama must've had on her phone. He's smiling but not at the camera, and his eyes look fuzzy. The email says he was last seen on our street. That he is recovering from a stroke and may appear to be confused. The alert makes me feel better and worse at the same time.

Malcolm gets home, and at first, he's all smiles, so I'm sure his meeting with the coach went well, but his smile evaporates when I tell him we need to drive around and look for Gee.

He frowns at me. "What are you talking about?"

I explain in as few words as possible what happened.

"You were *asleep*?" he accuses me. The question drills into my heart. "You told me you'd watch him!"

"I know!" I say, close to tears. "I did. I *was*." How can I explain I stopped sitting with Gee because I was doing this terrible thing to Aubrey?

Malcolm's hands clench and unclench, and a muscle in his cheek does the same thing. "Look, it's not your fault. You're sick. I shouldn't have gone. This was my responsibility."

His words come out like someone else gave him these words to say, and they make me feel 100 percent worse.

The front door opens, and I get less than a second to hope it's Gee before Mama storms in. She lights into Malcolm before I can stop her. Before I can explain anything.

Mama angry is a hurricane. She grabs the front of Malcolm's sweatshirt and shakes him.

"Mama!" I shout. "Mama!" I don't want her to throw that anger at me, but I can't just stand here and let Malcolm take it. "It wasn't his fault. I was supposed to be watching."

Mama narrows her eyes at me. "You're a *baby*. No one with any sense is gonna leave you alone to watch your grandfather." She turns back to Malcolm, releases him. "Boy, what were you thinking?"

"I'm sorry, Mama," Malcolm says. He doesn't tell her how it isn't his fault but mine. "I know I messed up. Can't we just go look for him?"

I want to ride in the car with Malcolm but Mama makes me ride with her. We drive up and down all the streets in our neighborhood, making a wider and wider sweep. After a while, I know we must be too far. No way could Gee have walked all this way. We pass a police car, and I check their back seat to see if Gee might be sitting there, but he's not. I want to see more police cars. I want to see an army.

"Someone will see him," Mama mumbles. Her eyes are anxious and flit back and forth, searching.

"Maybe we should go back. Maybe the police have found him," I say.

"They would've called," Mama says. She's had me check her phone every few seconds. No calls from the police, but tons of messages from her sisters and brothers. They are all out looking too.

We drive around for almost two hours before Mama pulls into a Perk Up! parking lot. "I need a cup of coffee," she says. As we're walking through the door, it must dawn on her that I'm supposed to be sick. "You probably need to get back into bed."

"That's okay, Mama," I say, not admitting to anything. "I want to be looking with you."

She nods and orders herself a large cappuccino and me some apple juice even though I told her I didn't want anything. "You need something in you," she says.

When they call her drink order, I think she'll take it and head right out to the car, but she sits down. "Where would he go?" she asks. I don't think she's really asking me. Just putting the question she's probably had rumbling around in her head all this time out in the air. But I still try to answer.

"I thought he might be trying to deliver mail. Like he used to. He likes doing that," I say.

Mama raises questioning eyebrows at me, so I explain the "game" Gee and I played delivering fake mail. Maybe I should've told her before now. Maybe she would've told me it was a bad idea.

But she nods and her eyes soften. "Daddy sure did like carrying that bag. June-bug wanted him to move to an administrative job in the office." Mama chuckles. June-bug is what she calls her mom. "Thought he should be a bit more respectable. But he liked being outside and all the people he met. All kinds of people."

I don't like how Mama sounds. Talking about Gee like he's not just missing but gone. "We'll find him, Mama."

She nods. "You know he was feeling so good when he first got up that morning."

I know what morning she means without having to ask. Saturday. The last day Gee was normal.

"We were talking about the name of your school, of all things. I think hearing those things about John Wayne the night before had him stewing some." Her eyes are sad, and I hope she doesn't start crying. I've never seen Mama cry, and I don't think I could handle it.

"He felt bad for holding on to the idea of the school being called John Wayne. Said he needed to set a better example for his grandchildren. Said it was important to celebrate the dream of equality. He wanted to make sure the name got changed, and he did get sort of riled up, but I never imagined . . ." Mama seems almost like she's talking to herself, but then she snaps back into the moment and really looks at me. "He really wanted you and Malcolm both to be strong. Tough." She smiles. "Like him. Not like me."

I'm totally shocked. I don't know anyone tougher than Mama.

She must read the disbelief on my face because she says, "Oh, you know I put on a good front. Hard as nails and can spit them out when I need to, right?" She snaps her fingers a couple of times, making the thin gold bracelets on her arm jangle.

I nod.

Mama rubs a knuckle between her eyebrows. "Lord knows y'all need to be strong in this world. Black kids get chewed up every day. Your grandfather knew that and made sure we all knew it too. When you were tiny, I used to carry you around everywhere. Whenever Daddy would see that, it would make him so mad. Kept telling me it didn't help you none to keep you soft." She takes a long sip of her coffee, then sets the cup down hard. Milky foam spouts from the sippy hole. "And after me and your dad broke up?" She shakes her head. "Whoo boy. I thought I was doing a good thing moving back home, but it sure gave him a lot of say in how I was raising my kids."

I lose Mama for a moment as she gets deep into her memories. A soft smile plays around her lips, but then she shakes her head hard and gets back to the moment.

"Him loving the Duke? Was all because the characters John Wayne played were tough but good, you know? He wanted to act like he didn't believe it, but hearing those bad things John Wayne said? That was hard." She takes another sip of coffee. "But you know my daddy is always going to stand up for what's right. He told me he was planning on going to the school board meeting. Wanted to show his support. But then he . . ." Her voice catches. I know what she was going to say. He was going to the meeting, until the stroke stopped him.

I sit up straight. I know exactly where Gee is.

"Mama," I say, "we gotta go."

59

BE SORRY FOR THAT

On the way to the school district office, I text both Malcolm and Aubrey. Only Malcolm answers. He'll meet us there. I keep throwing sideway glances at Mama, thinking about all the things she said.

"I'm sorry, Mama," I say, and I'm surprised how good it feels to finally say it.

Mama, misunderstanding, says, "This isn't your fault, Jenae. Malcolm should've been there, and even though Gee is still recovering from a stroke, he knows better than to go wandering off."

"No, not for that," I say.

"For what, then?" she asks, looking confused.

"For . . . you and my dad getting divorced." I hang my head. "It was because of me." I tug at my bottom lip, pinching it hard between my thumb and finger.

"Girl, what are you talking about?" Mama scoffs. "You're the *only* good thing that came out of me and Kamal. That relationship was a disaster from day one."

"But . . ." Didn't I make him go away? "I thought—"

"Me and that man fought every day we were together. Having you just added a spice to the stew. And trust me, if it hadn't been for you, we would have split a lot sooner. You kept us together for more years than was probably right." She laughs. "If you wanna be sorry for something, be sorry for that."

Then she reaches over and gives my knee a squeeze.

When we get to the district office, I'm surprised to see a huge crowd outside. You'd think there was going to be a concert or something. It's not until we get closer, and I see how mad a bunch of the people seem, that it's obvious this is not an excited crowd but an angry one.

My brother's so tall, he's easy to spot, and he waves me and Mama over. I bite my lip hard when I see Rox just behind him. I don't know what I'll do if she starts yelling at me, but she just gives me a small worried smile.

"We haven't seen him," Malcolm says, and my heart sinks a bit.

"But"—he waves his hand, indicating the crowd—"we haven't made it inside yet. Someone said they stopped letting people in because it was getting too loud. Supposed to open the doors back up when the name change comes up on the agenda."

"It's a mess out here," Rox says, and Mama does a quick look back-and-forth between Rox and Malcolm, but she's too worried about Gee to stop to ask questions about their relationship.

"We need to get inside," Mama says, and I agree, even though I don't know how we're going to do it.

The crowd is getting hyped up. People are waving signs

around, and a man is shouting through a bullhorn about John Wayne being an icon and about tradition. He's dressed like he came right off a set shooting a Western, and most of the people shouting along with him are in cowboy boots and some have cowboy hats on. I guess they're dressed like that so everyone knows they are supporting the Duke.

There's another group that's just in regular clothes, and they are shouting about representing our community. They're angry too. And they also have signs. About diversity. About respecting history. And they wave pictures of Sylvia Mendez.

The school district office isn't close to our house. It's hard to imagine Gee walked all this way, but I know that's what he did. And got here early enough to be one of the ones already inside. I just *know* it.

While we're waiting, all my aunts and uncles arrive. Mama texted them before we left the coffee shop, telling them to head to the district office, which meant she believed me. Instead of them continuing to look other places, they are all counting on me knowing where Gee is. He has to be here.

The crowd outside starts to get shouty.

The people standing outside of our school hadn't seemed angry; they just seemed like they were on different sides. But they're not like that tonight. Maybe because tonight it *matters*. If Tía Rosalie was right, tonight the school board is going to put the name change to a vote.

A man in a too-skinny tie and a rumpled shirt addresses

the crowd. "Okay, we're going to open the doors," he says. His voice trembles.

"There's probably not enough room for all of you. My . . . my staff is handing out comment cards. If you don't get in, don't worry, we'll still read your comments." He runs a nervous hand through his wavy hair. "Let's all be respectful," he says, but it almost sounds like a question instead of a command.

The doors open, and everyone ignores him and starts pushing to get in, and I'm glad I'm with my family because they sure don't let anyone push *us*. We move through the crowd as a blob, taking no prisoners. Malcolm uses his crutches to push people back. No way is anyone stopping us from getting inside. Not if Gee's in there.

And there he is. As soon as we make it in, I recognize the back of his head. Sitting almost in the front row. Straight and stiff as a board. And the head next to him is familiar too. Tía Rosalie.

"This fool man," Mama mutters, and then rushes down the aisle to him. "Daddy! Daddy! What were you thinking?" Her voice carries throughout the room. Mr. Humphries wouldn't need to teach Mama a thing about projection. We all follow her and crowd around Gee, even while Skinny-Tie Man tries to herd us back from the front.

The school board members have been discussing something, but with the commotion right in front of them, they all shut up and stare. I bet they're worried that the fight over the school name has flowed into the room.

Gee stares at us like he's never seen us before. His eyes fall on me, and I cringe. He looks angry. Maybe he's mad that we found him.

Tía Rosalie looks back and forth between our family and Gee. "You didn't know he was coming here?" she asks, glaring at Gee. "Oh my goodness. I'm so sorry!" She says something about helping, and giving Gee a ride, but most of it gets lost under Mama arguing with Gee.

"Come on," Mama says, trying to pull his arm. "Let's go home." She sounds angry, but I know it's all the worry she had boiling up inside her.

Gee doesn't budge. So she pulls harder on his arm.

I have to make her understand. "Mama, he wants to be here. For *Sylvia*."

Her eyes flit to the school board members and then back to Gee. I bet she's thinking about how Gee hasn't said a word since his stroke. And how there's no good reason for him to be here. Especially not after scaring us half to death.

"Please," Skinny-Tie Man says. "I need you to move to the back. You're blocking the aisle."

"Mama," I say. "Come on."

Mama gives up, and we all move back.

I scan the crowd for Aubrey. Even if he can't forgive me, I expect to see him. To care enough about this meeting to want to see what the school board decides, but he isn't here.

A board member says they would like to make a motion. They say they would like it resolved that the name of John Wayne Junior High be changed to Sylvia Mendez Junior High.

I think this is it. They will say okay or not, but instead someone announces there is a motion on the floor and it's now up for debate. At the word *debate*, I get a sour taste in my mouth.

The board starts talking about the name change. They talk about how much money it will cost and whether the district can afford it. They talk about process and policy. And they talk about the real stuff. The reasons we are all here. It's all the same arguments we've heard. Respecting history. Respecting the community.

It's not until a board member with a little *president* sign in front of her calls for public comments that anyone says anything about John Wayne making racist comments. I can actually see the wave that goes through the crowd. A tidal wave. There's all sorts of mumbling going on, and the board president asks for people to be quiet so they can hear the speakers.

Person after person gets up and says something. Sometimes for, sometimes against, but I don't think anyone on the for side says what they need to. No one talks about how important it will be, not for the neighborhood, but for the *students* at the school. But to me, that's more important than anything. If our school is named after Sylvia Mendez, then everyone at our school, everyone who ever goes to our school, will know about her. Will know that a kid can be brave.

I wait for Gee to get up and go to one of the mics they have in the aisles. That's why he's here. But he doesn't move. Does he think the words won't come? *Come on, Gee.* Then I think it harder. *COME ON, GEE!*

As if I shouted it at him, he turns and looks at me. He scowls. I point to the mic. He points at me.

At me.

60
NOTHING COMES OUT

"We'll just hear a few more comments before closing for the vote," the president says, sounding like she has a big headache.

Gee is watching me.

I walk toward a mic on my shaky legs. With each step, my tongue grows, making it hard to breathe. And my mouth is so dry, I can't swallow. A pain burns behind my left eyebrow, and I rub at it, trying to quiet down the heat, but that only makes it worse. My vision is starting to blur, and sweat drenches my shirt. I can't do this.

One of the board members points at me.

Everyone is watching.

They all see me.

Wait for me to say something.

I open my mouth, but nothing comes out.

The board member who pointed at me has turned away. She starts talking to the member next to her, and then the whole group is talking, but I can't hear a word. Blood and panic pound in my ears.

My legs are rubbery, and I don't know how I can make it back to my spot.

Suddenly, Gee is there, next to me. He grips my elbow. And at first, I think he's offering a supporting arm so I can walk to the back of the room without falling, but then his grip tightens. The blue circling his irises glows like ice.

I glance back at Mama, and she's watching me, looking like she's holding her breath. And then she does something I sure don't expect. She plants her feet wide, pops her hands onto her hips, and straightens up tall, with her chin raised and her eyes staring like daggers. She's striking Astrid Dane's trademark power pose. What Astrid does when she's about to

do something brave. And then Mama nods at me and smiles.

I open my mouth again.

"Wait," I say, and move closer to the mic. "Wait. I have something to say."

The whole board turns to look at me.

61

SOMETHING TO SAY

"I'm eleven years old and not very big, but I'm older and maybe bigger than Sylvia Mendez was when she had to go to a school where she wasn't wanted. Maybe every day the other kids said mean things, but Sylvia had to go anyway."

I think of Mr. Humphries's advice and take a big breath.

"I guess she was pretty scared. I don't know how anyone, especially a kid, could be that brave. And it seems like it's important . . ."

Everyone is staring at me. Everyone. My throat tightens.

"Important for other kids to see that. Real courage, not fake movie courage."

I feel Gee's grip on my arm tighten. "Gee—my grandpa— loves the Duke's movies. He watches them all the time. But just because someone was great at one thing doesn't mean we ignore their bad parts, and John Wayne said some stuff that wasn't nice. And if the Duke was the type of person who wouldn't have wanted someone like Sylvia Mendez at the same school as his kids, or wouldn't have wanted someone like me there, then maybe he isn't the best person for our school to be named after.

"I don't like giving speeches," I say. "I know it's hard for other people too, but not like it is for me." My scalp is sweating and I am pretty sure I stink something awful. "But my grandfather told me that life isn't supposed to be easy, and sometimes you have to overcome your fear if you want to do something great. If Sylvia Mendez could be so brave, then so can I. And that's why our school should be named after her."

When I am done, I hear some angry shouting, but mainly I hear the applause. Someone whistles, and when I look in the crowd to find out who, I see it is Mr. Humphries! And he isn't alone. Some of our class is here too. But Aubrey isn't.

I'm the last person who gets to make a comment, because Skinny-Tie Man nods at the school board president, and she leans toward her mic.

"Okay. Okay," she says. "On the motion of changing John Wayne Junior High to Sylvia Mendez Junior High, how do you vote?"

It's like a movie.

"Yes."

"Yes."

There's some applause, and the school board president tells everyone to please be quiet again.

"No."

That gets applause too, and my stomach starts to ache. I walk back to Mama, and she holds my hand.

"Yes."

"No."

"No."

It's a tie. The school board president has the last vote, and I'm trembling, I want this so much. I stare at her. Hard. So, so hard, and I beam one word at her: *YES*.

62
DECISION, DECISION

The president looks at me and rubs her index fingers around on her temples. She seems tired and like she has had a very long day, maybe a very long year. I wonder if she heard my thought blast.

She clears her throat and leans toward her mic. "On the subject of changing the name of John Wayne Junior High to Sylvia Mendez Junior High . . . I vote yes. The motion passes." She bangs her gavel, and just like that, it's done.

A glorious feeling spreads through my chest, and I jump up and down. We did it! I think over and over. It's like fireworks going off inside me. Malcolm comes over and gives me a high five and then squeezes me into a hug. His crutches rub against my shoulder, but I don't mind. Mama gives me a hug too and whispers into my ear that she's proud of me. Even Rox hugs me.

My aunts and uncles crowd around, while Skinny-Tie Man tries to get the crowd to leave the room.

Uncle AJ puts his arm around me.

"Look at you," he says.

"My, my, Jenae," Auntie Jackie calls out. "Aren't you something!"

My cheeks heat up, but I don't disappear. I'm not sure what I think of all this notice. It's awkward but not awful.

"Too bad that little friend of yours isn't here," Auntie Maug says.

I look around again for Aubrey, certain that if he's here, we can move past today. And somehow, we can be friends again. But I don't see that flame of hair anywhere.

63

SAFE BUT NOT SOUND

When we all get home, I don't know what to do with myself. I keep checking and checking my phone, but there aren't any messages from Aubrey. I text him that we found Gee and tell him again that I'm sorry, but he still doesn't reply. I can't even feel good about Rox and Malcolm sitting close to each other on the couch, laughing about something. I'm glad they are getting along, but it doesn't seem as important anymore. Not when I don't have anyone to share the news with.

I text Aubrey that I'm sorry, but I've already texted that a whole bunch of times, and he didn't answer any of those messages.

Everyone is so glad Gee is safe and sound that they all ended up over at our house, and it feels like a Friday.

The doorbell rings, and I race to it, knowing it's going to be Aubrey, but it's not.

"Jenae!" Tía Rosalie says. She's carrying a container of pastries. "I wanted to drop these off. And to say how sorry I am to have caused so much worry." She looks at me. "But to also say gracias. What you said at the meeting . . . so lovely. And *strong*. I was so proud of you. Your mami—you take after her."

"Thanks," I say, happy and disappointed at the same time.

Mama comes up behind me and asks Tía Rosalie to come inside, and with a surprised look, Tía does, handing me the pastries as she passes by.

"You should've left a note for your family, no?" she asks Gee disapprovingly, but then she gives his shoulder a little push to show she's teasing him.

"Right?" Mama says. "Acting like people wouldn't be scared to death." She and Tía Rosalie laugh together like they've been friends for a hundred years.

I watch everyone look so happy, and I want to be happy too, but I want Aubrey to be here.

I leave the pastries in the kitchen and then climb up the stairs. They groan like they always do, but this time they sound like they are groaning at me.

Up in my room, I text Aubrey again. I check my laptop to see if maybe he emailed me, which would be strange but not impossible. There's an email alert from the police department, letting everyone know Gee was found, but no mail from Aubrey.

I try watching an Astrid Dane video, but I can't focus on it. Everything in my room seems wrong.

All the talking and laughing from downstairs slithers into my room, and I find a playlist on my computer that Malcolm made for me. It's the perfect music for my mood, and I pop in my earbuds and fill my head with loud, angry words, drowning out everything else.

I keep glancing at my phone, beaming thoughts at it.

TEXT ME BACK.

TEXT ME BACK.

But my phone stays silent.

64

FIXING EVERYTHING

In the morning, I feel sick, which is pretty ironic. But no way am I going to ask Mama if I can stay home. Sometimes you just can't avoid your problems.

The drive to school is too fast, though, and before I want to be, I'm walking into first-period history.

I take my seat next to Aubrey and try to smile hopefully at him, but he doesn't even look over at me. This is going to be harder than I thought.

It's still so early in the school year, maybe I could get my schedule changed. Swap English and history. That would fix everything.

When the bell rings at the end of class, instead of walking out, Aubrey goes up to talk to Mrs. Crawford, and I wonder if he's asking if he can change desks. Or maybe he got the idea too of switching classes.

I pass behind them, and neither of them glances my way. I am invisible.

At lunch, I go to our spot and hope Aubrey will show up.

I can't imagine what made me think eating lunch by myself, away from everyone, was ever a good idea. It's pretty horrible now.

I can't even eat. Everything tastes like sand. And no matter where I look, I don't see bright red hair.

After lunch, I trudge my way to English.

A moment after I sit down, Aubrey comes in, and we lock eyes for a moment, but then he looks away, and I stare down at my desk.

Mr. Humphries quickly takes attendance, and then he scrapes his chair back and stands up. He walks to the front of the class, giving stern looks to anyone who hasn't settled down yet. "Good afternoon, class. Today we are—"

I shoot my hand into the air, and Mr. Humphries stops talking in a jerk, clearly surprised that I, of all people, would be interrupting him. I'm shocked myself. I look up at my arm and wonder how it got up there.

"Yes, Jenae?" he asks. "Do you need to go to the bathroom?"

My tongue starts to swell, and I pull my Astrid Dane bag to my chest. I didn't take any books out yet, and the weight of the bag is a tiny bit comforting. "No. I need to say something."

Mr. Humphries blinks in surprise. A few people are looking at me like a horn just sprouted from my forehead.

"What would you like to say?"

"Just that . . ." Yesterday was hard with a bunch of strangers looking at me; this is ten times worse. "Being in this class has been hard for me," I say, and my voice is barely above a whisper.

"I even tried to transfer out of it." My throat has shrunk down to straw size. Everyone is staring at me now. I have never felt so visible. I don't know what to say and hope that if I start talking the right words will come. I think about my breathing and fill my lungs.

"Yesterday I let down my . . . my friend. I was afraid. I thought if I had to give a speech, I might die." The class titters at that, and I smile self-consciously. I swallow and notice my tongue has shrunk down almost to normal size.

"Anyway," I go on, "I wish I hadn't messed everything up. And I think everyone deserves second chances. And I know you said no makeups, Mr. Humphries, but maybe you could make an exception." My voice has gotten so quiet, I'm not sure if anyone heard me. It's hard to talk when you have tears ready to gush up your throat and fill your whole head, until they spill out of your eyes and nose onto the floor. "That's all I wanted to say," I mumble.

"Well, Jenae," Mr. Humphries says, "I, for one, am very happy you chose to stay in our class. And although you make a good point, we just don't have time in the schedule for makeups."

"Okay," I say sadly. I pull out a notebook and flip to a blank page. I try to take notes on everything Mr. Humphries says as if I'm truly listening.

Before class is over, an eighth grader, Javier, comes in with a piece of paper. He hands it to Mr. Humphries, and after Mr. Humphries reads what's on it, he tells Javier he can go back to his class. Then Mr. Humphries says, "Well, the eighth graders met at lunch and picked two students who will join debate club this year. Before I announce the names, I should mention the debate club members gave full consideration to everyone who gave speeches." Mr. Humphries pauses and looks over at me. "Whether their partner showed up or not."

A tiny gasp slips out of my throat. Is Mr. Humphries saying what I think he is?

"It wouldn't be fair to punish someone just because their partner didn't deliver a speech," Mr. Humphries says, and I wish he would either stop saying *partner* or would just say my name. Everyone knows who he is talking about.

"I'm pleased to announce the students who are joining the club are . . ." Mr. Humphries pauses like we're at an awards show and he needs dramatic effect. I just need him to hurry up and say Aubrey's name.

I thought blast as hard as I can at Mr. Humphries. *AUBREY BANKS!* No matter what's on that paper, that has to be one of the names Mr. Humphries is going to call. I'm so relieved I didn't mess things up for Aubrey. Maybe now he will forgive me.

"Dawn Hernandez and Joshua Chin!" Mr. Humphries calls out.

The room tilts. There must be a mistake. I wait for Mr. Humphries to call out another name.

"Okay, everyone, make sure you study your vocabulary words," Mr. Humphries says over the bell. "There will be a test tomorrow. And, Aubrey, can I speak to you for a moment?"

I walk to sixth period feeling like I'm moving through molasses.

Right now Mr. Humphries is probably telling Aubrey that they couldn't really judge Aubrey without me being there. Aubrey is going to hate me forever.

Not even math helps today, and when I leave school to head home, I'm not surprised there's no red-haired boy waiting for me.

The street seems oddly quiet with all the protesters gone. The banner saying SYLVIA MENDEZ JUNIOR HIGH is back, covering the John Wayne sign, and I guess this time it will stay up.

I walk slowly, wondering how I'm going to get through the school year.

"Jenae!" a voice shouts. "Jenae! Hey, Jenae, wait up!"

I turn around and see Aubrey running toward me, and a whole bunch of people staring. Whatever. Let them look.

When Aubrey reaches me, he's all out of breath. "Have you seen it?" he yells at me.

I don't know what he's talking about. "Aubrey, I—"

"The video? You haven't seen it? On YouTube?" Every question is a shout.

He must be talking about a new Astrid Dane video, and I don't even care. "Please, Aubrey, we need to—"

"Just check!"

"Fine!" I take out my phone.

He huddles close to me, and when I type in Astrid Dane in

the search, he grabs my phone away.

"No! Here, let me." He types in something else, and a video starts.

But it's not Astrid Dane. It's me.

At the school board meeting. Giving my speech.

When it's over, he says, "I can't believe you did that. And you're on YouTube. Like Astrid Dane." His voice is full of admiration.

We both are staring at my phone, even though it's now playing some random video about turtles. My mouth feels glued shut, and inside, the words are twisted up like a bird's nest. I turn off the video and put away my phone.

"Me speaking up at the school board meeting doesn't change what I did," I say sadly. "What I *didn't* do, I mean." Each word feels heavy.

"But what you said in class does," he says, and shuffles his feet. He gives me a quick glance before looking away again "You didn't have to do that. I know how hard that must've bee for you."

We look straight at each other, and I know for sure t Aubrey really sees me. But I see him too. "It was hard. But have to," I say. "Because of me, you don't get to be in the de club, and I knew how important that was for you."

"About that," Aubrey says, and starts twisting his hair. know what Mr. Humphries told me after class?"

I shake my head.

"He knew I really wanted to join the club, so he wa

let me know why they didn't pick me. Instead of arguing the side of keeping the name, I argued the other side. Because that's what I really thought, that the name should be changed. But I hadn't prepared for that side, so it was just a lot of me sort of . . . shouting? I—I didn't *really* do a bunch of debates in Chicago. I sort of did pretend ones in my room. And the camp was a virtual one online. But I thought I was pretty del." He says the last word hesitantly and blushes. "Mr. Humphries showed me the video of you to let me see what a good speech about calling our school Sylvia Mendez Junior High would look like. Sort of funny that if you had showed up to school and given that speech, *you'd* be in the debate club now."

There's nothing funny about that. "But if I had been there, you would've given the speech you prepared. So you might've been picked."

Aubrey shakes his head. "It was my fault for switching. I shouldn't have done that." He gives me a shy look. "I *was* mad at you for not coming to school. Like you got mad at me for not telling you about being homeschooled and everything. I should've answered your texts, but there was a bunch of times you didn't answer mine. And I was really upset and I just needed . . ." He almost smiles, but it's not his big face-eating smile. It doesn't reach his eyes. He's talking slow and enunciating everything extra careful, like he wants to make sure I understand him. "I guess to think about things? I knew you felt bad, but I wasn't ready to forgive you."

I'm not sure if he's saying he *is* ready now.

"Or maybe I wasn't ready to admit I was wrong too."

At my questioning look, he goes on.

"You tried to tell me. You told me you couldn't do it. I didn't listen. And that's not how a friend should act. At least I don't think so. Honestly, I don't have much experience. Maybe we should make a pact to tell each other the full honest truth all the time, and to listen to each other?"

I nod. It sounds like what friends should do. "So we're . . . okay?" I ask, barely speaking above a whisper.

"Click," he says.

If it wouldn't be spectacularly weird, I think I would give him a gigantic hug.

65

FINISH WHAT'S STARTED

It doesn't take us long at all to get to my house, and we're not even through the front door when I hear the television. It's blaring like usual, and Gee is sitting in his chair snoring, and Malcolm is on the couch connected to his knee-bender machine.

At first, I'm disappointed, because it seems like nothing has changed.

Aubrey and I step all the way inside and I shut the door firmly behind us.

Gee's eyes pop open, and he holds his arms out, and I quickly close the gap between me and his chair and deliver a loud kiss to his cheek. And I tell him what I've been wanting to say for what feels like years.

"I'm sorry," I whisper into his ear. Malcolm and Mama and Aubrey don't think it's true, but I know what I know. Sometimes thoughts really can hurt someone.

Gee swipes at his ear like I'm a mosquito. He clears his throat and opens his mouth, but nothing comes out.

"Don't worry," I tell him. "You'll talk when you're ready."

The front door opens, and Mama walks in, her face a thunderstorm. "Jenae Monique Dorrian! Did you ask your father to get you out of school yesterday?"

My happiness blows out like a candle. I had forgotten all about that. "Mama, I'm sorry." I glance over at Aubrey. I don't want him thinking about how badly I worked to get out of school.

"You're gonna be sorry, all right," she says, her voice hard steel.

"Oh, Mama, chill," Malcolm says. "The dude didn't even do it."

Before Mama can argue and get on me about faking sick, Malcolm asks her, "Do you want to hear about my plan or not? You've been steady asking me. Now's your chance."

Mama glares at me, but then she sets down her purse and keys. "Go ahead, then. Tell me," she says to Malcolm.

"Well, I wanted to tell y'all yesterday after I met with Coach Naz, but there was a bit of drama going on."

"Malcolm, will you please just tell me what's going on?" Mama asks, sounding exasperated.

"I'm going back to school. I'm not going to be able to ball, obviously. At least not this year, but yeah. I'm going. That's my plan."

"'Bout time you came to the right decision," Mama says, but she doesn't sound angry anymore. She sounds relieved.

"Registered this morning. The quarter starts Monday," Malcolm says, "so I'll need to fly out this weekend."

I feel like there are a million butterflies in my belly. "I'm going to miss you," I say.

Malcolm pats the spot next to him on the couch, and I go sit down, and Aubrey plops down next to me. We put our matching Astrid Dane bags on the floor.

"I'll miss you too," Malcolm tells me. "Just like before."

I'm sort of shocked. I didn't really think Malcolm missed me at all.

"So let's hear it," Malcolm says. "What was your worst thing?"

"Oh, not this foolishness," Mama complains.

I think about all the bad things that happened lately. Which was worst? Mama clears her throat, and I can guess what *she* thinks is the worst thing. I know for sure I'll be hearing about a punishment later, but right now, I just shake my head.

"Okay, then, what was your *best* thing?" Malcolm asks, smiling at me. There's a lot on that side too. Maybe more.

"A seagull didn't poop on my head," I say, and my smile is so big, I swear it's about to eat my whole face.

Mama slides out of her high heels and says, "Girl, you are seriously odd."

"Yep," I agree happily. "I'm not like anybody else." But then I think, except maybe, sort of, I'm a little bit like the strange boy sitting next to me.

Gee makes a sound that could be a cough or him trying to say *Quiet down!* He waves his hand at the television, and I can almost hear him yelling about trying to watch his program.

"Sorry, Gee," I say. "We won't say another word."

As she heads to the kitchen, Mama says, "Why don't you put on that foolishness you like. It'll do Daddy some good to watch something from this decade for a change."

Aubrey and I say at the same time, "It's not foolishness!"

"Two of you." Malcolm shakes his head.

"Yep," I say, and look at my friend with his flaming-red hair and smile as vast as an ocean. "Two of us. Click."

ACKNOWLEDGMENTS

My vision for this book was always difficult for me to describe. There was so much I wanted to do (Art! There needs to be art!) and complicated things I wanted to say. I worried that no one was going to get it. I'm so grateful I got to tell this story my way.

One of the things I love about publishing is the moment when I move from the very solitary time of drafting a novel to being part of a team. I am blessed to have a *great* team. My critique partner Jenn Kompos always knows exactly the right thing to say. My awesome agent, Brenda Bowen, is a great coach and source of so much wisdom, and my editor, Alessandra Balzer, is simply incredible and continues to make me such a better writer with gentle (but strong) nudges and suggestions. And thank goodness for the copy editors who make sure I get my facts right—talk about unseen and unsung heroes! So many others brought this book to life, but a huge shout-out of thanks to Nicholle Kobi, who brilliantly brought Jenae to life on the cover, and Bre Indigo, who just blew me away with her ability to illustrate my crazy creation—Astrid Dane.

Thank you to everyone at Balzer+Bray/HarperCollins, especially Caitlin Johnson, Patty Rosati, Mimi Rankin, Stephanie Macy, Robby Imfeld, and Molly Fehr.

I'm so grateful that sensitivity reads are a thing and that this book benefited from a strong expert read. (That being said, if there are still problems, the fault is mine alone.) Even with the best intentions we can get things wrong, so having someone point out areas where I can do better, is such a blessing. Speaking of experts, thanks, Dr. Chris, for answering my pediatric leukemia questions (and apologies for anything I got wrong). Thank you to Camille and Steph, who gave me insight into dealing with a basketball injury.

Thank you to my wonderful critique group: Sally, Kath, Lydia, Stacy, and Rose. I talk a lot about how great they are at providing input and insight, but maybe more important is the laughter they bring to my life and their constant support through the highs and lows.

Thank you, Nic, Sabaa, Angie, Keely, Lindsay, Karen, Mariama, and Alicia. You all are not only amazing writers but also so quick to offer your time and support, and are so willing to answer my many, many questions. Huge thanks to Renée Watson, whose amazing guidance in a workshop at a Kweli conference brought a pivotal scene to life. I also so appreciate the nice things you said about the book!

My SOTYs, my coworkers, my NorCal writing community, and my zumberas are so hugely, incredibly supportive, it truly blows me away. Special shout-out to Christy Jane and Angela for just being incredible. Thank you, Alice, for making sure I stay sane at work, and I'm not sure where I'd be without

Griff, who stands by me through it all and allows me to be completely, utterly ridiculous.

Biggest, hugest thanks to my family. They encourage and support me every step of the way. Thank you, Keith, Morgan, and Jordan; your love and belief in me mean the world. Thank you, Mom, for being proud of me no matter what. Jimmy, Pam, and Linda thanks for celebrating me as if I were a big shot when I am still simply your baby sister.

Thank you to the readers out there who have written me and let me know how my words have touched them. That is the very best part of this whole journey.

Finally, thank you, God, for always being there. I sure have needed you.